SELFLESS

Fated Mates – Book Six

Lilli Carlisle

ALSO BY LILLI CARLISLE

FATED MATES

Tigress

Huntress

Speechless

Merciless

Fearless

THE BLACK RIDGE WOLF PACK

Omega's Choice

Ceva's Chance

Karli's Resolve

Laura's Legacy

Lili's Trust

Katrina's Destiny

www.BOROUGHSPUBLISHINGGROUP.com

SELFLESS
Copyright © 2021 LILLI CARLISLE

ISBN 978-1-953810-53-3

This has been possible only with the love and support of my family.
Love you Craig, Samantha, Katie, and Jason.

AUTHOR'S NOTE

Thank you for following along on this journey with me. We've traveled through a world where humans became a commodity. The shifters humans had been hunted, and most shifters didn't know the hybrids existed until they were called upon to save what was left of humanity. Old beliefs and new biases threatened to derail everything they'd accomplished, but by the grace and compassion of five goddesses, truth reigned supreme. Now they are on the cusp of launching an offense on the demons to regain control of the earth. Through their trials, they've learned they were stronger as one, and leaving behind old beliefs and judgments from both sides is the only way to carry on and avoid extinction.

I look forward to seeing all of you come along for the next bunch of romantic adventures in my newest series *Gods & Thunder*.

Love, Lilli.

SELFLESS

Chapter One

Hope quietly shut the children's bedroom door and tiptoed back into her kitchen in the bunkers. She'd dreamt about having a chance at relaxing and reading her book this evening, but they'd run out of jam. In normal circumstances, you could run to the store, but they weren't living in normal times considering Collector Demons had taken control of the earth's surface less than five years earlier. Instead, she stared down at the container of strawberries working on a plan to get at least six jars of jam out of them. The children loved strawberry jam.

Her vision blurred and a searing pain shot through the right side of her head again, but this time with little to no warning. Typically, she'd had a few seconds after losing her sight before the pain struck. Not this time, though.

"Not again," she growled in frustration.

She held onto the kitchen island, squeezed her eyes shut, and waited for it to pass. Over the last few months, these pain-filled episodes had become more frequent, making them harder for her to ignore. She didn't have time for this.

The pain spread through the back of her head and settled in her eyes like daggers piercing her eyeballs. Shifters didn't get migraines if that was indeed what this was. There was no logical reason for this to be happening to her. She was a bear-shifter, strong and tough to the bone. Unfortunately, Hope felt anything but that. Her body shook uncontrollably as beads of sweat rolled down her back. This had to stop.

Several moments later the pain mercifully began to fade, and her vision slowly cleared. She picked up a glass that was sitting on the counter and filled it with cold water before gulping it down. Hope took a few moments to collect herself before she laid out the strawberries, sugar, lemons, canning jars, and pots. She was about to start crushing the washed strawberries when someone knocked softly on her front door.

Hope set the container down and went to see who it was. It wasn't late by anyone else's standard, but when you have two active youngsters with an eight o'clock bedtime, her exhausted body felt as though it might have been midnight in her world. Hope brushed her hand through her hair and straightened her clothing, no need to look as retched as she felt. Didn't need to draw attention to herself and risk having the children taken from her care. They were a family, and she'd be damned if she'd lose another one.

When Hope turned the corner leading to the living room, she could see who was waiting through the glass sidelights of the door. Gareth. Her heart rate sped up, but she put that down to her anger at the tiger-shifter's hovering. Her friend Sarah had asked Gareth to watch over her, Jenny, and Matthew when their underground facility came under threat of collapse due to a broken ventilation system. However, their new homes were safe once again thanks to Sarah repairing the system, and the danger had passed, but Gareth was still here, and no matter what she did, the big tiger wouldn't leave. Of course, he'd returned to his job, maintaining the machines keeping their underground city running, but in all his spare time, Gareth could be found right here, hovering.

Hope hung her head and opened the front door. "The children are in bed, Gareth. All tucked in safe and sound. Now go away." Okay, so maybe she was a bit testy.

"Good evening, Hope," Gareth said while retaining that damn grin of his. "I came to check on you."

"I'm as fine as I was the day before and the day before that." The guy never gave up. "I'm making a few jars of jam before heading to bed myself."

"Jam," Gareth said with a big smile. "I'm great at crushing things." He stepped in and walked past Hope, heading straight for the kitchen.

"I bet you are, but I don't need any help." Hope felt she'd been saying that a lot over the past few weeks.

"Tsk, tsk. You're still not done reading that book?" Gareth asked as he pointed at the novel sitting on the coffee table and effectively changing the subject.

"I'm a little pressed for time if you haven't noticed." She was so damn tired.

"That's why I'm here," Gareth said as he picked up her book before bringing it over to her. "You hold this," he said as he gave her the book before leading her over to one of the two armchairs in the living room. "And sit here while I get this jam production underway."

Before Hope had time to stop it, she was sitting in her chair with her book in her hands while Gareth took over her kitchen. When she tried to stand, he waved his index finger at her as if scolding a child, and she'd be damned if she didn't sit back down. What was wrong with her?

"You work hard all day, so this is the least I can do considering I eat here so often." That was as good a reason as any.

"You wouldn't eat here so often if you'd simply stay in your area of the bunkers." Simple and true, if not a bit concerning.

"This is my part of the bunkers," Gareth chuckled as he began crushing the strawberries with the potato masher.

"What?" Why were her ears suddenly ringing? Hope feared her headache would come barreling back, and so far, she'd been able to keep her attacks private.

"Yeah, I'm moving into the apartment beside you and the kids," Gareth said with a grin.

"You're doing what? Why?" Hope struggled with the fact that she was equal parts excited as angry. "This is the restricted area. People are sent here. It's not a move into any time kinda place." The restricted area housed the humans, hybrid human-shifters, and those who cared for them and their mates. It was restricted to all others to ensure an easier transition for them into the underground bunkers and shifter society.

"The triads agreed by me moving closer, I could help you and the kids more." He honestly acted as if he'd won some sort of prize.

She didn't need help with the children. Hope was about to stand when the electric kettle began to whistle on the counter. When had he put that on?

"Ah, your tea will be ready in a moment," Gareth said as he expertly navigated her kitchen. Soon she was tucked into her chair with a book, herbal tea, and blanket while Gareth added the other ingredients to the pot of strawberries. The man moved fast.

Hope wasn't a push-over by any means, but for some reason, when it came to the tiger-shifter she was more likely to give in.

He mixed the crushed strawberries with the sugar and then put the mixture to a boil on the stove before adding the lemon juice and a bit of the zest from the lemon.

"How do you know how to make jam?" Hope asked. It wasn't something she would suspect a large, male tiger-shifter to know.

"Single fathers learn a lot out of necessity," Gareth chuckled. "You'd be amazed at what I can whip up with only a few ingredients."

Hope knew Gareth had raised his two sons on his own for many years, not knowing his daughter, Matriarch Raz, was alive. However, she wasn't privy to the entire story.

"You raised them alone, and from what I hear, they're doing great among the pack Enforcers." Hope gave credit where credit was due. It couldn't have been easy after his mate died. Mates were essentially an extension of one's own being. The bond was that strong.

"Yes. Thankfully, both my sons and daughter have found their place among the pack. Their mother would be immensely proud of all three of them." Gareth smiled wide when he spoke of his former mate.

"I'm sorry your mate couldn't be here with all of you." It must be crushing, losing a mate.

Gareth's smile turned both melancholy and reflective. "Thank you. So am I."

"What was she like?" Hope asked, praying she hadn't taken a step too far, but by Gareth's returning smile, he didn't seem to mind.

He continued to stir the boiling pot full of jam as he got this far-away look on his face. "Mara was my light and life. My mate could brighten any situation with simply a smile, the same as Raz does now. She reminds me of her mother every time I look at her. On weekends, I remember we'd pack everyone up and head to one of the lakes on tiger lands and let the kids run free for the afternoon. Raz was just a cub and Cormac and Connor young adolescents back then. They loved to play in the water."

"Sounds wonderful." She fondly remembered days like that spent with her parents. They always used to laugh when they pulled out their picnic basket. Having lived through Yogi and Boo-Boo cartoons where the bear is always looking for a 'pic-a-nic' basket to swipe.

"It was perfect," Gareth agreed as he began transferring spoonsful of jam into the mason jars. "Seems like yesterday, but it's shocking to say we lost her over fifty years ago."

"Time marches on for all of us whether we want it to or not." Hope understood that fact more than most.

"Yes, it does, but thankfully I was able to find Raz still alive after all these years," Gareth nodded as he spoke.

"How did you get separated?" Hope asked, again hoping she hadn't asked too much but too engrossed in the story to stop herself.

Gareth set the jars off to the side before twisting on the lids. "The same man that killed Mara. It was her insane ex, and my sons' biological father. He took Natalie—better known now as Razelle— and we never saw her again. After years of searching without a sign or any word, we assumed the worst. That is my failure. I should have kept looking." His tone changed by the end of his explanation to a more subdued and reflective tone.

Hope regarded Gareth in a slightly different light. He was still pushy, annoying, and overbearing, but she'd give him a little leeway, it wasn't as if his life had been perfect either.

"What happened is not your fault. That crazy bastard did that, not you." She couldn't let him blame himself for such evil. "You cannot take responsibility for everything."

"That crazy bastard won't be doing anything to anyone anymore." Gareth's voice took on a menacing tone along with the odd growl. Hope saw the glint of revenge in Gareth's eyes. In their world violence was a given. They shared their lives with animals, after all. Here the term 'an eye for an eye' took on profound meaning.

"Good. May he rot in hell," she said. "Things have a way of working out sometimes. You found Raz, and from what I can tell, you have a strong father-daughter bond with her."

"And my granddaughter, Asta." Hope watched Gareth's face light up at the mention of the toddler.

Hope couldn't help but smile at the thought of her as well. She had hair the same color as her mother's and grandfather's, orange with a bit of light blonde and black stripes. Asta would turn up as a tiger-striped wolf or a grey tiger since she'd started shifting. She was a mixture of her parents. "She is one adorable little girl."

"I'll bring her by so she can play with Jenny and Matthew, if that's okay with you?" Gareth offered.

"I think they'd enjoy that," Hope accepted. It would be good for them to play with someone new. "Anytime."

As Gareth rotated the filled mason jars in the hot water bath, Hope could feel the weight of the day slowly sinking in and her tired eyes closing. Jenny and Matthew had school lessons to complete today, and Archie, their golden retriever, ate two cushions from the loveseat. She'd cooked three meals, sorted snacks, had playtime, bath time, and clean-up time, and spent an hour trying to convince Matthew that bouncing between his and Jenny's bed wasn't safe. It had been a full day, even for a shifter. Most were, but she'd never give it up. Jenny and Matthew were hers to care for and raise. Her little family.

Gareth continued to talk about a repair he'd completed today directly on top of the facility. Their new home was underneath a mountain range and only accessible by a complex, well-guarded cave system. They'd been underground going on five years, but before that they lived among the humans hiding in plain sight. They worked and owned businesses to help support the pack, clan, or any shifter group. That was before the Collector Demons arrived, destroying much of the above ground world with them.

Millenia ago, in the time of the pharaohs, the same demons had attempted to destroy this world, but five goddesses joined forces, both shifter, and human, to fight this new invader and send them back across the veil separating the worlds.

Only, this time around, the demons had a new plan to take over this world and make it their own instead of incinerating it. After the first war, demons had been weakened so much that to possess a body, the human's soul had to be already essentially evil or at least that's how it used to be before they'd gathered enough souls to exert more pressure on a human's willpower.

History had shown their deeds through world wars, catastrophes, and acts of terrorism as the demons wore their human shells to effect results in the human world. The more death, violence, and destruction they wrought, the more their strength grew. Now they could travel across the veil any time they wanted and could once again possess human bodies at will. Thankfully, shifters couldn't be possessed since they shared their souls with an animal, and neither could human children because of their innocence. But for how long was anybody's guess.

Over the centuries, humans forgot about the day the demons were driven back. History explained it away in fairy tales and myths even though their shifter images were chiseled onto the same walls as the great kings of Egypt. Most humans lived their entire lives not knowing shifters existed, and the ones who did hunted them mercilessly.

Jenny and Matthew were safe but would never be able to return to the surface as long as the demons ruled society. The Collector Demons kept humans like livestock, using them as their very own power cells when they needed a new body or to recharge one already taken. Their host bodies decayed much slower this time around, allowing them to have control over the shell for longer periods.

They used a machine that Sarah, Marie, and Ben's mother, Joan, had been unfortunate enough to experience. It sucked the energy out of a shifter to give the demons themselves better shelf life, for lack of a better term. Now shifters were hunted and caged along with the humans, across the globe, all shifter species had gone to ground to avoid them.

The human hunters were no longer in control. They worked for the demons to keep themselves off the menu along with certain groups of hyena-shifters. The world above them had collapsed, and with it, all semblance of normal society. The ruins of cities and towns littered the earth, quiet and deadly if you were caught out in one.

So far, three goddesses have emerged in this fight; reincarnated in Raz, Rose, and Zahra. Everyone prayed the remaining two would appear soon so they could fight back with more effect and retake the earth, sending the Collector Demons back to the hell they sprang from.

Hope hadn't been to the surface in what felt like forever, and she wondered if she or the children would ever see it again in their lifetimes. As a shifter, she had a better chance, living to over one thousand years, while humans had eighty to ninety years on average. Hope missed the feel of real sunlight on her face and the breeze heavy with scents, rushing through her hair.

Her head rested back against the cushions. She wasn't sure, but she'd swear she'd never been as comfortable as she was right now, or that could have been the exhaustion talking. Whichever it was, it wasn't long before Hope drifted off to sleep with images of her family home left above ground to rot and fade away in time, taking the last piece of her family with it.

***

Gareth repeated his story for the third time to make sure Hope was sleeping deeply. He'd already taken the remaining jars out of the pot and turned off the stove. He'd kept the same monotone voice throughout his explanation, hoping to settle an exhausted Hope. When she'd answered the door, the dark circles under her eyes were unmistakable. So, he jumped in to help.

He'd been away from her and the kids for the entire day running maintenance checks on the external sensors. Gareth liked to do them often to reassure himself they were working properly. He didn't like the thought of uninvited strangers showing up. The only drawback was once you started, you had to go through them all, and there were hundreds of sensors.

That had resulted in him only making it back to the restricted area well after supper when the kids were asleep. He'd tried his best to get there before bedtime, but the quick meeting he'd been called to attend on his way back from the surface, wasn't as speedy as he'd hoped. The meeting was important, considering it involved him moving into the restricted area closer to Hope and the kids. Now the triads had agreed with his request, all that was left to do was move his belongings over and be settled by the morning.

Gareth double-checked the stove was off, cleaned up the area in the kitchen he'd been using, and turned to Hope, who was still sleeping soundly, sitting up in her chair. He couldn't leave her in that uncomfortable position, so as slowly as possible, he plucked her book out of her open hand, slid his arms underneath her back and knees, and lifted her from the chair and over to the couch.

He didn't think they were at a spot in their relationship where he could walk into her bedroom and lay her on the bed, so this would have to do. The blankets lying over the back of the couch came in handy, and soon he had her bundled for the night as she remained sleeping.

With one final look, he brushed a stray brown curl away from Hope's beautiful face, headed for the door, and turned off the lights. He still had a long night before him if he wanted to be moved in and possibly get a few hours of sleep as well. He shut the door softly, and when he turned away from the door, found Sarah waiting for him by the patio chairs in the center of the darkened courtyard. The lighting corresponded with the actual sun was helpful to most to keep their rhythms synced.

When he reached her, he sat and said, "Good evening, Sarah."

"Hello, Gareth," she replied. "How is Hope today?"

"I was only able to see her for a short time while I was finishing up with jarring the jam."

"Jarring the jam?" Sarah asked with one platinum blonde brow arched. "Is that some sort of code for sex?"

"What? No," Gareth choked. "Hope was making a batch of strawberry jam when I arrived, so I took over, and she fell asleep in her chair. I moved her to the couch before I left."

"Good, at least she's resting," Sarah said without even a hint of embarrassment. "Earlier today, I noticed she appeared to be in severe pain. When I asked her about it, she said it was nothing. Have you seen this happen?"

"I've noticed the same thing happen a few different times this month. However, when I tried to bring it up, she reminded me she doesn't need my help, and I'm free to leave at any time."

"Avoidance," Sarah stated.

"Definitely. But how do we convince Hope to see Doctor Jewel if she won't even admit there's something wrong?" Gareth worried about her day in and day out.

"Well, if she won't go see Jewel, then we'll bring the doctor to her," Sarah said with a no-nonsense tone. Sarah was an albino hyena-shifter who'd been rescued from the demon hordes. In the end, it turned out Sarah had saved the entire facility with her ability to command metal and other matters. If it weren't for her, all the shifters, human-shifter hybrids, and human children would have lost their new shelter less than a year of being underground.

"This isn't going to end well, but I agree." Hope needed to have this checked out.

"You let me worry about that," Sarah said before standing. "Don't you have some moving to do?"

"I stopped to talk to you." Gareth shook his head at the audacious hyena. "Are you always this pushy?"

"Only when I have good to do." Sarah's grin said it all.

Gareth chuckled. "Well, I have to admit you do it well."

"Thank you, I try. Now be gone."

"You women are going to be the death of me," Gareth chuckled and stood.

On his way back to his old apartment, Gareth ran possible scenarios through his mind. Jewel shows up, Hope loses her mind and banishes him. Jewel checks Hope out and finds something wrong. This one scared him the most. Then there was the old standby – Hope goes furry and throws him across the courtyard. Every scenario sucked, but he cared for her and had to get her some sort of help, whether she saw it that way or not.

Chapter Two

"Why do we have to have checkups?" Jenny huffed as Hope helped her pull on her flowered shirt.

The little girl loved flowers, and whenever Ben and Marie came across an old fabric store on recon missions above ground, they'd bring back floral and airplane prints for Hope to sew into clothing for both children. Matthew had seen an airplane on an old rerun and had fallen in love with them ever since. Matthew had been hiding under a seat on one of those double-decker buses while London burned around him. So when Matthew showed an interest in something she did everything she could to foster it.

Luckily, their group thought ahead and downloaded as many television programs and movies as possible before the fall of society. There would be a need for entertainment being underground for however long it took to reclaim the surface.

"Because we want to make sure you are growing and healthy," Hope explained for what she thought might be the twenty-fifth time in the last half hour. "I love you guys and want you to be happy and healthy."

"We love you too," Jenny said before hugging Hope. Another pair of arms announced Matthew had joined in. He still hadn't spoken a word since they'd rescued him in London, along with Ben and Jenny.

Hope never pressured the little boy to talk. She figured after seeing what these children had seen, Matthew could talk when he was good and ready. As for now, they understood each other fine, and that would continue until Matthew chose another way of communicating.

A wet tongue licked up the side of her cheek, assuring her that Archie, their golden retriever, felt the same way about their little family. Archie was a rescue as well from one of the missions.

"Okay, you two, let's go eat our breakfast while we wait for Jewel to arrive," Hope said while throwing their nighties into the laundry hamper. She'd have to make time to get a couple of loads done today.

Hope had found it a bit odd that Jewel would contact her so early in the morning about coming by to perform mini physicals on the children, but she understood the need to keep up on their health checks. There were hundreds of different possible mental links between shifters, private, mate only, triads, family members, anyone. When Hope had mentioned being contacted, she meant Jewel spoke to her through their mental link. Something she was sorry the children would never be a part of.

Jenny and Matthew were human and susceptible to human illness, whereas shifter children had their healing abilities from birth. That fact scared her the most. They were so fragile compared to a shifter child causing Hope to be on alert twenty-four-seven in case they were hurt, came down with a cough, or anything really.

The children sat at the breakfast bar attached to the island and dove into their scrambled eggs, bacon, fruit, and jam-covered toast. Hope was about to put her eggs into the frying pan when there was a knock on their front door.

She leaned around the partial wall to look, and sure enough, it was Gareth.

"Come in," she yelled. "How do you want your eggs?"

He walked into the kitchen without saying a word, took the spatula from her hand, and led Hope over to an empty chair beside the children. "I want them prepared by me while you relax."

Hope couldn't help but laugh at his antics. No matter how overbearing Gareth was, he was always charming. "Well then," she said while winking at the children. "I'll have eggs benedict with hollandaise sauce and a mimosa."

Gareth didn't even blink an eye. "Do you have English muffins?"

"Seriously? You'd prepare that for me?" Hope wasn't sure if the resourceful man meant it, but if last night's jam performance meant anything, it was possible.

"If you want it, yes."

Hope still couldn't get a read on Gareth. Was he doing this out of some misguided duty to an oath he swore to Sarah when their new home was under threat, or did he honestly like being around them and their chaos? Well, considering the way it all went down, she imagined she'd never know which one it was. Too bad.

"I was teasing. I'll have scrambled, please." Hope said and thought back to the moment she met her new 'protector.'

The children, Archie, and she were waiting for their turn to be teleported away by a goddess to the partially built second facility. They were again evacuating their homes, but this time it wasn't from demons; a shifter saboteur took out their ventilation system. Suddenly, this huge tiger-shifter came up to her and introduced himself as her new bodyguard. Hope wasn't entirely certain what to call him, but one thing was sure, he never left her side through it all and now made himself a frequent visitor.

"It's scramble time," Gareth announced like some commentator at a boxing match, making the children laugh. The two had grown attached to the big guy and looked forward to the times he was here with them.

Soon she and Gareth had heaping plates of breakfast goodness sitting in front of them, and they began eating while the children, having already finished, went off to play in their bedroom.

"So, did you manage to get your belongings moved last night?" Hope asked, not knowing why she needed that answered first.

"Yes, all settled," Gareth said once he swallowed his mouthful of scrambled egg. "Even managed to get in a couple of hours sleep."

"Oh, yes, that reminds me. Thank you for moving me to the couch last night. I can't believe I fell asleep on you like that. Sorry." Hope felt horrible for dozing off during their conversation, but the solid night of sleep she got was so needed.

"Sorry? Sorry for what? Being tired?" Gareth asked. "Of anyone here, you deserve to rest when you can. You never stop. You're always doing something for someone. What about you?"

"What about me?" Hope asked while pointing her fork at herself. "This is how I choose to live."

"Caring for everyone but yourself," Gareth pointed out. "Never a moment to relax."

"I'll have you know I enjoy helping others." Hope had been that way for so long that she couldn't imagine any other way of being.

"I'm not saying you should stop. I'm just pointing out that you need some 'me' time every so often. I could watch the kids. They like me," Gareth offered. "Take your bear out for a walk on the fields' level and relax. Roll around on the grass under a real tree."

Before Hope could come up with an excuse to avoid his offer, there was another knock at the door. "Come in. Join the party."

Jewel entered carrying a small bag, which undoubtedly held her instruments to check the children's health.

"Good morning, everyone," Jewel said as she joined them in the kitchen.

"Morning, Jewel," Gareth said. "Want some breakfast?"

"No, thank you. I've eaten already."

"Morning," Hope started to clear away the dishes. She'd wash them after the children had their checkups. "Jenny, Matthew, Jewel is here. Please come out to the living room."

Gareth stood, taking the dishes from her hands. "You go with the kids in case they're scared, and I'll clean up in here."

Hope relinquished the cutlery and headed toward the children. No questions were asked. If the tiger wanted to do the dishes, so be it. She'd always choose the children to anything else offered. That was probably why she had so many chores to do after the children went to bed.

Jenny and Matthew sat on the couch, looking ready to bolt at any second as Jewel took a few items from her bag. The usual things: a stethoscope, that rubber reflex hammer thingy, and the light they use to look in your ears. Hope wasn't a doctor and didn't pretend to know what their proper names were.

"It's okay, guys, those won't hurt you," Hope said as Jewel pulled out two small syringes. Seriously?

Both children took off like the hounds of hell were on their heels, straight out the front door and away into the courtyard.

"Sorry," Jewel said as she quickly put the inoculations away. "I wasn't thinking."

Hope stood and ran for the door. The children had already made it a quarter way down the courtyard with Archie by their sides. Hope knew she could easily catch up with them with her shifter speed, or mainly because they were under four feet tall, but that's not how she wanted to do this—forcing them to submit.

So instead, she sat down in her favorite patio chair and waited. Others living in the restricted area came from their apartments to see what was going on. Sarah and Joseph came out while Sarah's newly rescued sister watched in her hyena form from the window. Hope would have to remember to bake more of her blueberry-nut pound cake for the traumatized hyena. She seemed to like it. Ben and Marie stood in their window, and Joan, Ben's mother, stood in the door to her apartment next door.

Jenny eventually looked back, and when she realized Hope wasn't following them, she pulled Matthew to a stop. Hope waited for them to choose, return, and have their checkup with regular human shots or refuse. In which case, she would accept that and keep an extra careful eye on them if they were ever near any humans. Shifters did not have diseases to pass to one another, so they'd be safe if the kids stayed around them alone.

After a couple of unsure moments, the children began walking back towards her hand in hand. Jenny had always been the leader of the two of them. Don't let her curly blonde hair fool you. She was older than Matthew by at least a year, considering Jenny had told them that she'd had her sixth birthday party.

When they were within three feet of her, the children stopped and formed a unified front, shoulder to shoulder. Hope couldn't have been prouder.

"We don't want to get needles," Jenny explained. "They hurt."

"I understand," Hope said in a calm voice.

"Are you going to make us?" Jenny was honestly a wonder, sharp as a nail, and able to comprehend well beyond her years.

"No."

"No?"

"Correct. I won't force you to have your immunizations."

Matthew and Jenny looked at each other in confusion, obviously expecting her to force them into it. "We can have the rest of our checkup. No ouches?"

"Of course, it'll be a shame, but I respect your decision," Hope said without emotion, not wanting either of them to know how much she needed them to have their scheduled shots.

Jenny's eyebrows furrowed, and her eyes squinted together. "Shame?"

"Yes, because you'll never be able to play with any other human children we find." Hope couldn't risk them. She felt horrible about it, but it was one or the other.

"Why can't we play with them?" Jenny asked while Matthew studied Hope's face as if looking for answers.

"Because you haven't had your shots to protect you," Hope explained. "We can never risk any of them bringing a human illness near either of you."

Hope watched as Jenny's child-mind worked it out. "They could make us sick?"

"Yes. That's why human children need vaccines to protect them. Shifters do not have such things as childhood diseases." They had decided when they first found the children to maintain a normal vaccine schedule to keep them safe. Thankfully, they were able to find stocks of medication for humans in different pharmacies when out on recon missions. "I love the two of you and only want you both to be healthy and happy."

The children stepped closer to Hope, and she held her arms out wide. Both ran into them, and she hugged them fiercely. Mine. She would do whatever it took to protect these two.

"Okay," Jenny said, her voice muffled against Hope's shirt.

"What, honey?" Hope asked as she pulled back a touch to look at them. She wanted them to be sure.

"We'll get our shots," Jenny said while Matthew nodded his head. "We'll be safe to play with other kids."

"Thank you for understanding how important this is," Hope said before kissing them both on their foreheads. "We'll make chocolate ice cream this afternoon to celebrate your very wise decision."

With an ice cream cheer, the children took her offered hands, and they walked back inside their home. "I'll be by your side the entire time."

"And Gareth?" Jenny asked.

"I have an even better suggestion," Gareth said out of nowhere. "How about Hope goes first? What do you think, guys? That way, you'll see there's nothing to fear."

Hope agreed that would be a good idea and a way to calm the children further, so she took the seat they'd set out for Jenny and Matthew.

With a wink towards the children, Hope said, "Lay it on me, doc." Both laughed as she had hoped they would. The last thing she wanted was for the children to be fearful of doctors.

Jewel went about all the regular checks and asked the normal question: How's your sleep. Any concerns? Before tying a rubber band around her upper arm and pulling out an empty syringe. Faster than Hope could even ask why, Jewel had it stuck in her arm and was collecting her blood.

"We always like to check on the health of our clan as well," Jewel explained before capping the needle and placing it back into her bag. "All done. See, that's not so bad. Right, kids?"

Jenny nodded. "I'll go first so Matthew can see again." Always the leader, making sure it was as safe as it looked.

Jenny sat straight in the chair, looking every bit the warrior headed for battle. Gareth came to stand beside Hope watching the little girl have her eyes, ears, and throat checked, along with a list of other things. All too soon, the needle was removed from Jewel's bag and uncapped, but instead of Jenny tearing up, the little trooper set her jaw, took hold of Hope's and Gareth's hands, and closed her eyes. A few seconds later, and it was over.

Jenny cracked open one eye and then the other, watching as Jewel placed a colorful bandage over the area. "All done. You did an amazing job, sweetie."

The little girl broke out in one of the biggest smiles and jumped off the chair, allowing Matthew to take her place. "It's okay, Matthew. It didn't hurt much." Hope respected that Jenny didn't sugarcoat it and added the word 'much.'

She and Gareth held the little boy's hands as he went through the same routine as Jenny had. When it came time, he closed his eyes as Jenny had done, and it was over. Matthew jumped out of the chair, ran his fingers over the bandage before raising his arms in celebration as if he'd crossed a finish line.

Hope gathered both children in her arms. She couldn't help herself. "I'm so proud of the bravery the two of you have shown here today."

After releasing them with accompanying kisses, they went to play as the three adults headed to the kitchen island.

"Coffee, anyone?" Hope asked, trying to keep her calm.

"No, thank you. I have a few more exams scheduled for today," Jewel answered without looking up from her tablet.

"So, how are they doing?" Most importantly, are the children healthy?

Jewel consulted her notes. "From what I've learned about human physiology, they are at the point they need to be for their ages in both height and weight relatively speaking, considering we don't know their exact birthdates. As for their health, I found nothing wrong with either of them. They are healthy and happy right here with you, Hope."

She couldn't help but smile back at Jewel in relief. That's all she ever wanted for them. "Thank you." Now on to more deceitful discoveries. "So, when do you plan on checking my blood?"

"Oh, whenever I get around to it," Jewel said as she waved her right hand in the air as if batting something away before glancing at Gareth. "No hurry."

Hope looked between them. "Do you both seriously think I'm that imbecile? I'll admit you had me up until you drew blood."

"What do you mean?" Gareth asked and Hope noted he was giving a performance that could have net him an Emmy in another time and world.

"'Let's have Hope go first,' bullshit. You didn't have to set me up by using the children." Hope didn't like that one bit. "Never use the children."

"They required their checkup and vaccinations, you know that," Jewel argued, not looking so sure as before.

"True, I'll give you that," she grudgingly agreed. "But you took it and used it as a perfect ruse to have a look-see in my head."

"I was worried," Gareth confessed, not in the least repentant.

"Because I get headaches? Or become tired sometimes? I'm caring for two continually active children. Parents have both of those symptoms, and no one calls in the doctor." You would think she had body parts withering away and falling off by their reactions.

"Please let the doctor help you," Gareth asked, and for the first time, Hope saw real concern instead of his usual cocky demeanor. "I'm asking as a favor to me."

"And if I pass all these tests, you won't bring it up again, correct?" She had to check because there was no way she was going through this every week.

"Yes, if Jewel gives you a clean bill of health, I will not bug you about your headaches again." Gareth's green eyes stared down at her with an intensity she'd never seen before.

"Fine."

"How long have you had these headaches, and how often do they occur?" Jewel asked in rapid-fire succession, perhaps afraid Hope would clam up before she was done with her questions.

"Five months, three to four times a week."

"That often?" Gareth gasped.

"Do you notice any commonality with what you're doing or ingesting when the pain strikes, and do you get any warning signs before it happens?"

"No, I haven't been paying too close of attention to what I'm doing, but I get about a five-second warning when my vision blurs. At least most times."

"How long does the pain and vision loss typically last?"

"Anywhere from ten seconds to a minute roughly." She held up her hand when it looked as if Gareth was about to interrupt.

"I'll need you to keep a log from this point onwards. Maybe we can find a connection. How bad is the pain on a scale of one to ten, with ten being the worst pain you've ever felt?"

Hope stopped and thought about it. Each time she felt the pain slicing through her head, it had been slightly different, as if testing her ability to take it or looking for a weakness. Great, now she was acting as if the pain were sentient. "Hmm, they're all different. One time it's hardly a two and over quickly, while others are closer to eight or nine."

"If it's possible, could you contact me when you have one of these episodes so that I can examine you immediately?" Jewel asked.

"I'm not having episodes. They are just run-of-the-mill headaches." She didn't want it to get out that she had episodes of any kind. Would she be declared unfit to care for the children?

"You're a shifter. You shouldn't be having headaches unless someone knocked you upside your head," Gareth growled. Hope knew he was frustrated by her lack of acceptance of anything being wrong, but she couldn't allow there to be.

"Fine, I will contact you if I have another one. Okay?" Compromise.

"Thank you," Jewel said. "I'll head back to the clinic and get started on your blood workup. If I find anything, I'll let you know."

The doctor left quickly, leaving Gareth a sitting duck. "You lied to me and used the children against me."

"I didn't want to, but your health comes first," Gareth began explaining. "You would have never gone to see the Doc yourself." True.

"Who are you to decide anything about the children and me? This oath thing with Sarah is getting out of hand." She couldn't have someone around all the time watching her every move and reporting it back.

"You still think that's the reason I keep coming around?" Gareth growled as one lengthening canine peaked through from under his lip. "Some damned oath?"

"Of course, that's why you're here in the first place." They both knew that.

"I admit, at the start, that was the case, but as I got to know you and the kids, I began to care about the three of you. So, sue me," Gareth growled, frustration mounting.

"Get out." Two simple words felt like a sucker punch even to her, but she wouldn't take them back.

"What?" he asked.

"I need to be alone for a while. I've had enough with the events of this morning and need quiet. Go to work, Gareth." She needed peace and time with the kids.

Gareth stood to his full height and huffed. "You want to be alone so bad; I'll leave you alone." He walked out the front door and closed it behind him without once looking back.

Hope leaned her head against the cool counter. What had she done? She was beginning to like having the tiger around, but fear is a powerful motivator. She couldn't let anyone find a reason to take her children away if she were found to be sick. Here was their home with her. Hope had to remain strong for the children. They'd lost too much already.

Chapter Three

He was an ass. Gareth was positive about that one thing. He'd lost his cool, and now here he sat in his new apartment staring at old reruns of nineties television sitcoms, having already watched the news reports from the day. The shifter population had set up their own global network since the fall of society and were able to keep track of the movements of the demons. It had already been three days since he'd stormed off, and he hadn't stepped inside Hope's home since.

He'd talked and played with the kids when they were outside and he was home from work, but other than that, he hadn't spoken to Hope. Gareth was too embarrassed he'd lost his cool making things exponentially worse than they should have been. Yes, he was frustrated and worried Hope wasn't taking her health seriously, but that didn't give him the right to storm out like that. He and Jewel ambushed her with the medical exam out of nowhere. Of course, Hope would need time to think through everything.

Was he hurt she didn't react when he said he cared about her? Sure, but that wasn't Hope's fault alone. What was she to think after he barreled his way into her life without asking? She worked hard every day to ensure the children were happy and safe, only to have a tiger-shifter come in and change the rules. How could he be so stupid?

None of this was on Hope. The failure was his alone, yet again.

The knock on his door brought Gareth back from his musings, and he stood to answer it. He couldn't see anyone through the glass sidelights, so he opened the door to find a plate heaped with lasagna, garlic loaf, and a big piece of chocolate cake sitting on a tray on the ground waiting for him. He looked out into the courtyard and only heard Hope's door softly closing as she went back inside.

He picked up the tray and carried the meal inside to his kitchen counter. He'd missed Hope's cooking. Everything looked and smelled delicious, and he found a piece of paper sticking out from under the bread when he was about to dig in.

Bring the plates back when you come for breakfast. Hope.

Gareth could feel his heart rate speeding up. Hope hadn't banished him as she so rightly deserved to do and was allowing him an easy entrance back into their lives. Hope was truly a generous and loving bear, and he'd happily take the second chance she'd given him.

***

Hope had never been so nervous making breakfast before. What was wrong with her? The tiger had her all screwed up inside. Did she want him to leave that day? Hell, yes. Did she mean to make it permanent? No. However, that seems to be what she got. She'd had to sit through days of watching him playing with the children with not so much as a glance. Her bear was furious with her. The stubborn fool had grown fond of the tiger since Gareth started coming around. Hope had let the fear of losing her little family consume her, causing her to lash out at a man who'd been concerned. The same man who had helped her on so many occasions she couldn't keep track and asked for nothing. *Yep, I'm an ass.*

The children had already cleaned their plates, and she was about to crack a couple of eggs for herself when there was a knock on their door.

"Come in," she called without even looking to see who it was. If nothing else, it would give her a few extra seconds to think of a way to apologize to Gareth, who was undoubtedly only a few feet away from her now.

She heard the door open and shut as she began whisking her eggs. Hope added three more in case Gareth was hungry after she'd finished explaining why she freaked out on him. When the footsteps stopped behind her, Hope gathered herself and turned around with a big smile for Gareth, only to find Sarah not him as expected, and she was holding a tray of clean dishes from her gifted dinner, standing a few feet away. For a moment, she felt something inside her snap before her vision blurred and pain ripped through her head, forcing her to the ground.

She could feel hands on her but couldn't see who it was. A voice was muffled as she fought to stand, but her muscles seized. When she tried to speak she bit her tongue and tasted blood.

After several seconds, her muscles relaxed again. "T-the children," she cried as her words slurred together. "Where a-are they? Keep safe." Lord knew she couldn't do it.

Strong arms lifted her from the ground as more voices joined the fray, but Hope still could not understand them. The pain was getting worse. She was beginning to feel light-headed and knew she would lose consciousness. Hope fought with everything she had to stay awake, but in the end, it made no difference, and her world went dark.

***

Hope woke to the sounds of an argument. Somebody was raising one hell of a fuss, and she wasn't surprised by who.

"Why is she still unconscious?" Gareth's voice rang out.

"We don't know," Jewel replied. "We've tried everything, and nothing is making any difference. Even the goddesses have tried to wake her."

"Well, she's awake now," Hope said, cutting into their shouting match. "How could anyone sleep with the two of you carrying on like that?"

"Thank the gods," Gareth huffed, his voice at a more reasonable level.

Hope reached up to touch her face and found her eyes were bandaged in cloth. "What happened? Why are my eyes covered?" But she asked the most important question loudest. "Where are the children?"

Hope tried to pull the cloth from her eyes, but it was secured too tightly. When she tried to sit up, hands pushed her back down.

"I swear I'm about to go furry," Hope warned. "So, unless you want to deal with an angry bear, someone better start talking,"

"Hold on, give us a minute. You had us scared there for a while," Jewel said from her left side as she began to work on the coverings.

Hope could scent Gareth to her right and reached for him. He took hold of her hand instantly and pressed the palm of her hand to his cheek. It was wet. Was her big, tough tiger crying? Her attention was quickly captured by the scent of a shifter child and blood not too far away from her. Why would a shifter child be injured so severely to warrant a visit to Jewel? The same as adult shifters, child shifters were born with the ability to heal most wounds all on their own.

"You were unconscious for so long," Gareth said, his voice cracking and recapturing her attention. "The kids are safe. I checked on them myself. They're with Marie and Ben at your apartment and can't wait for you to come home."

Hope let out a deep breath. Jenny and Matthew were safe. "They must have been so scared."

"I spoke with them, and they understand you're sick and need to get better," Gareth explained.

"I am better. I'm fully conscious and without a single pain to speak of. So, if you would take this cloth off my eyes, we can go show them." She wanted to get back to them quickly.

Silence.

"Guys?"

Gareth took her hand that he'd been holding and pressed the palm to her cheek. That's when it hit her that the dressings covering her eyes were gone. Frantically, she ran her hands over her face and found her eyes were open. She could feel her body begin to shake and was powerless to stop it from happening.

"I can't see. Why can't I see?" Hope asked while throwing her arms wide, desperate to touch something solid with her hands. She found Gareth and held on tight.

"The goddesses are on their way," Jewel explained, offering a chance that their powers could fix this. "When you arrived here in the infirmary, you were unconscious, and upon checking your pupils, I noticed your eyes had changed color."

"Changed color?" Could this get any worse? "What color are they now?" Bears' eyes were typically brown to amber.

"They're a stunning silver, Hope." Gareth's voice was strong, exactly what she needed right now.

"Silver, great, so nothing even close to brown. Not only am I blind, but my eyes are freaky." Then the real problem hit her. "The triads will take my children from me because I'm blind."

With her enhanced shifter senses, she heard several footsteps headed their way and by their scents she knew the triads had arrived and likely heard her previous comment.

"Many blind individuals are outstanding parents," Raz, the wolf matriarch and goddess, said from somewhere to the right. "We would never take the human children from you, Hope. They love you as a mother, and that is how it will stay."

Hope could feel her speeding heart slowing down to a more normal rate and let her head rest back against the pillow. She didn't know what she'd do if Jenny and Matthew were taken from her, but she was prepared to go all Momma Bear on anyone who tried.

"How are you feeling, Hope?" Rose, the bear matriarch and goddess asked. Her concern was evident in her voice.

"Physically, I feel fine. No more pain, at least, but I can't see, and my eyes have changed color. How could a headache cause this?" Hope was getting nervous. Could this be permanent?

"Let's admit right from the start that these weren't simple headaches. And as a bear-shifter, your body should be able to heal itself," Goddess Zahra stated from the foot of her bed. The goddess could communicate through thought because she'd lost the ability to speak thanks to a former evil alpha triad.

Hope was able to place each individual even though she couldn't see them. Raz, Axel and Xander; along with Rose, Mason, and Riker; and Zahra, John, and Jewel. Shifters, the same as the animals they share their lives with, have exceptional hearing and smell, which would be helpful if the goddesses' powers didn't work to heal her eyes. It had to work. She couldn't be a blind bear, not now in these times of danger. She had to protect Jenny and Matthew from the Collector Demons and their henchmen, the human hunters and hyena-shifters.

"Yes, I admit they were out of the ordinary," Hope huffed. "But it wasn't something I couldn't take until now."

"We were researching the cause shortly before Hope fell unconscious. Her blood work is normal, and there was no sign of a nerve agent," Jewel explained.

"Nerve agent?" Hope asked. "Why would it be from a nerve agent?"

"There are those among us who are still unhappy about sharing the bunkers with humans. Along with the fact that we had a saboteur in our midst who almost destroyed our home…we're leaving our options open," Raz explained.

"They're only human children?" Her voice was raising. "No one would attack children?"

"Yes, but they might aim at the children's caregiver and you must remember some shifters have lost their own children to human hunters. Family members, entire packs decimated by those hunters. It's hard for some to put that aside when they see Jenny and Matthew."

"So, you thought maybe someone was trying to poison me? Did you check the children?" Hope wanted out of this bed so that she could find her children and protect them.

"Yes, don't worry. No one has attempted anything with the children. They are safe and will remain so," Rose assured.

"Let's not get carried away with something that never was. There is no threat, and you are completely free of anything that could have been introduced to you through food or drink. It's like asking for trouble," Axel said, the wolf alpha and one of Raz's mates, and Hope wholeheartedly agreed.

"So, let's see what we can do about your eyesight," Raz announced, and Hope felt people moving around her bed. However, Gareth not once let go of her hand, and she was thankful for that even though he'd refused to come for the apology breakfast, sending Sarah instead with her dishes.

Hope felt a warmth spread through her body, and she was positive, if she could see, the goddesses' hands were glowing above her as they used their gifted powers to help her.

Just as suddenly, Hope's ears began ringing, pulling her back from her relaxed position. For some unknown reason, the warmth she felt earlier turned into fire and shot through her body like lightning. She wasn't in pain, simply shock. Seconds later, everything stopped. No warmth, no lightning, nothing. Hope could sense everyone except Gareth had moved away from her bed. He continued to hold her hand tight. He hadn't abandoned her.

"What happened? What's going on?" she asked, strengthening her hold on the determined tiger-shifter's hand.

"Well, it seems you now have some sort of defense mechanism," Gareth explained.

"Defense for what? How? Did I hurt anyone?" This was getting worse by the second. She couldn't see and somehow, she was dangerous to those around her.

"Everyone is fine, but we must have set it off while we were trying to heal your eyes," Zahra said. *"I wonder if it would go off if anyone tried something against Hope?"*

"Like an alarm in a car? I'm not a car." Panic was setting in. Her brain may no longer hurt, but it was now filled with a thousand questions.

"No, but it is security, nonetheless," Jewel stated analytically. "It lit your body up with bright silver bolts of lightning running all over your skin. It was a clear warning."

"Will you please stop talking about this as if I have another being inside me. My bear and I are quite happy alone." Yes, she was freaking out.

"Sorry," Jewel said. "Sometimes my professional curiosity takes over."

Now she was a curiosity. Damn. "If you can't do anything for me right now, I wish to leave and return to my home." The children must be freaked out, and she desperately needed to hold them.

Silence.

"I know you guys are discussing it through your private link, so you might as well say what you're thinking out loud," Hope growled. She wanted everything out in the open because she couldn't see their faces.

Shifters could have complete conversations with other members of their clan or pack through thought alone. It was a simple matter of blood exchange, usually by pinprick on a finger for new members or by mating bite. The triads were able to keep track of every member, which came in handy in these battle conditions.

"Are you sure that's a good idea," Riker, the clan's Beta, and one of Rose's mates said. "What if this happens again?"

Hope went on alert. He was suggesting she was a danger to Jenny and Matthew. No, this couldn't be happening. Her bear began growling inside as she struggled to hold her control over the beast.

"It only happened when we tried to repair her sight. Considering no one else has that ability, I doubt Hope is a danger to anyone," Rose explained.

"True, I agree," Zahra said. *"Home would be the best place for Hope to heal while we try to figure out the cause of this change."*

She'd never harm the children. At least never intentionally. Shit, now she had that worry stuck in her head.

"You would never harm them," Gareth whispered as the others discussed her fate. The members belonging to the bunkers had a common mental link allowing them to communicate to others even with large distances between them. This ensured pack safety and security. However, she hadn't sent her thoughts to him but wasn't ready to split hairs right at this moment, so she set that aside.

"Thank you," Hope said and pulled herself together, borrowing strength from the powerful tiger-shifter.

"I won't hurt my children," Hope growled to get their attention. "I wish to go home."

She could sense Raz getting closer to her. "We all know you would never do anything like that. We were merely concerned in case your new powers return. We aren't sure how far this protection will go."

"Powers? More like a curse. Why would I have powers?" She was plain old Hope who no one ever notices unless they needed something. Sad truth.

"I'm not entirely sure what's going on, but I have no doubt, had we continued, your new powers would have stopped us. I don't think we've seen the end of this change," Raz said.

"Change? Great, I'm a lab experiment. Is it possible I could have caught something?" Okay, even she had to admit that was a stretch. "What use are powers if I'm blind?"

The word kept echoing in her head: blind. Her entire world had been turned upside down yet again, and as always, she had zero say in it.

She was getting tired of that being the case.

Chapter Four

Gareth held onto Hope as she navigated the steps down to their living level in the restricted area. She'd refused when he'd offered to carry her, which wasn't a surprise to him. Hope was strong and independent, and Gareth expected her to have getting around the apartment down in no time. This whole scenario had him and his tiger going into a hyper-protective mode, which he doubted Hope would appreciate. All the cat wanted to do was wrap her up and lock her away somewhere she couldn't be hurt. Sometimes his tiger went overboard. On Raz's suggestion, he and Hope had exchanged a pinprick of blood so that they could communicate privately. This would make Gareth her temporary eyes until the goddesses could fix them.

"Okay, so two more steps, and we'll be on our level," Gareth instructed while holding Hope safely in his arms so she didn't fall.

"Got it. Ten levels down from the infirmary," Hope said as she made the final few steps. "Two-hundred and forty steps."

He wasn't surprised by the number. "Exactly. Now we're turning left and walking down the corridor." All areas were carved out of earth and stone and covered by layers of steel. Gareth led her until they reached the gates to the restricted area. "We are at the entrance to our home. In front of you is the courtyard."

"Where are the kids?" Of course, they were her main concern.

Gareth looked up, and sure enough, Jenny and Matthew had spotted Hope and were running in their direction. "They're on their way."

"Okay, don't let me fall in front of them, please," Hope said as Gareth watched her gather her strength around herself. It was apparent she didn't want to show the children any weakness.

"I would never let you fall," he said. "But the kids would understand."

"Thank you, Gareth," Hope said as she patted his upper arm. "I know they would. It's just that I don't want them to worry I can't protect them."

"Hope," Jenny yelled before wrapping herself around Hope's legs while Matthew did the same on the other side of her. "We missed you. Marie told us you were sick and had to get better. Are you better now?"

"Almost. I'm on the mend, little ones. I missed you both terribly while I was gone." Hope lowered to her knees as Gareth kept her steady and gathered them both into her arms.

"Why are your eyes funny?" Jenny asked with the innocence of a child.

When Hope didn't immediately respond, Gareth stepped up. "Hope's eyes are still healing, so we'll have to help her until her sight has returned. I think they're beautiful."

Jenny put her hands on either side of Hope's face as Matthew looked on. Gareth could feel her anxiety skyrocket through their pack/clan link. After a few tense moments, the little girl smiled. "They are pretty, and they shine. I like them. Can we have hamburgers for lunch, Hope?" It amazed him how quickly children could adjust.

"Yes, sweetheart. I'll get them ready once we're all settled." Hope's voice broke with emotion as she pulled the two closer.

"Yeah," Jenny cheered alongside a bouncy excited Matthew.

Hope stood, and Gareth took hold of her right hand while Jenny held onto her left, and Matthew ran ahead with a huge smile on his face. He could feel Hope's joy returning as they were joined by Marie and Ben, who'd been taking care of the children while she was away.

Marie was a bear-shifter while Ben, her mate, was a hybrid human grizzly rescued along with Jenny and Matthew. Zahra had been given the gift of sensing the human-shifters who lived hidden among the humans before everything went to hell. They shared their existence with animals even if they didn't know it so couldn't be possessed like full humans.

"It's so good to see you on your feet again," Marie said. "You had us worried."

"Almost good as new, except for my eyes," Hope responded cheerfully, but Gareth could sense her worry.

"Yes, we were told that your sight hadn't returned yet," Ben said. "But I'm sure the goddesses will discover the cause soon."

"I agree," Marie said. "They've been able to do many amazing things. Not that it's going to take something amazing to return your sight. I'm sure they'll have you fixed in no time. Not to say that you're broken, but…"

Marie was falling all over herself, trying to be assuring without saying something wrong. Gareth understood there'd be a learning curve as people got used to Hope's new normal.

Hope raised her hand towards Marie's general direction, and when the other bear-shifter took it, she said, "I understand what you meant, Marie, and thank you for taking care of the children while I was gone. You two have been lifesavers and so good to the children from the start."

"If you need anything, we are here for you," Ben said. "We'll give you guys some privacy to get settled back in."

"Thanks again, guys," Gareth said before leading Hope towards her open front door. She had taken the time to decorate the front of her apartment's metal bunker walls like a brick house, including a pseudo front porch with rocking chairs. Marie had mentioned that Hope's above-ground family home had been similar.

Out of earshot, Hope whispered, "That was painful, but who can blame them."

"Everyone will get used to the change," Gareth said, trying to be reassuring. "Besides, the goddesses will figure this out in no time."

Once inside, he closed the door and helped Hope sit on the couch where Jenny and Matthew flanked her instantly. Their bond was strong, and he wanted to be a part of it, but now his main concern was to help Hope adjust.

"So, I heard something about hamburgers," he said, making both children cheer. "I happen to be a master griller."

"Yes, please," Jenny said, without moving away from Hope. "With ketchup on top."

"There should be some ground beef in the fridge if it hasn't already been cooked while I was gone," Hope instructed. "Buns are in the freezer, so they'll need to be defrosted."

"You got it," Gareth said as he opened the fridge and took out the ground beef. "The meat's still in the fridge."

He set about making lunch as Hope and the children spent some much-needed time together, talking and cuddling on the couch. The love the bear-shifter and her human children shared couldn't be denied. Not so long-ago, Gareth would have never imagined that occurring. This new world came with many adjustments, but Hope stood as the shining example of what could be accomplished between humans and shifters.

By the time he was ready to put the burgers on the indoor grill, he looked over to find Hope walking around the living room with the children's help as she counted her steps. So far, she had taken this blow well, much better than anyone could have expected, but he wondered when it would all hit home for her. When the emotional stress and fear would overtake her rational, organized attempts to exert control over her world again.

Gareth prayed he was here when the time came to support her and help her through it. He'd already received a leave from duties by the triads so that he could be here when she needed him, and he could help her navigate through the darkness. Gareth wished he could do more to help Hope get her sight back but that was for the goddesses and the doctor to figure out. Ask him to protect and defend something, make a five-course meal, repair any of the security monitors, and Gareth could do that without issue. Action he understood and would prefer it over this unknown enemy attacking the person he'd fallen in love with. If there was a way he could help, Gareth swore to find it. Until then, he'd make this transition as easy as he could for this small family, no matter the cost.

***

Hope didn't know how long she could keep this up. It had been days since she'd been released from the infirmary, and she still had no answers as to why she was now blind. Although there was one welcome side effect. She hadn't had a single headache since the one that took her sight. This left her to wonder if something had snapped in her head that last time. The episode had been painful enough to do some damage. She'd tried shifting back and forth from her bear, but it made no difference to her sight.

Five paces to the right. She counted them off and then continued forward past the couch on her way towards the kitchen. *Ten paces forward.* By the change in the sound of her feet against the flooring, she knew she'd stepped from carpeting to tile, indicating she was in the kitchen. With her left hand slightly ahead of her, she felt for the door handle of the fridge.

Hope was thirsty and didn't want to bug anyone to get her a glass of juice. Anyway, the kids, and Gareth were in the courtyard playing with Archie. She slid her hand along the stainless-steel fridge and brushed against the handle. Once she had the door open, Hope felt the different containers Gareth had chosen to help her organize objects in her mind.

Small circular plastic containers were for sauces and dips. There were medium-sized rectangular for meats and proteins, milk was in a ceramic jug, while juices and waters were in taller plastic jugs. Of course, more things needed to be added, but that would come in time. It helped to have her bear's enhanced senses when identifying what was in her hands or near her. Hell, she could scent anyone entering the restricted area, which calmed her knowing she wouldn't be caught unaware.

When her fingers brushed against a tall jug, Hope felt for the handle and lifted it out of the fridge. She could smell peaches, which was fortunate considering they'd made peach juice that morning.

Five paces left. When she reached the fifth pace, she held out her hand to touch the cupboard hanging over the counter. Inside she felt around for a glass, brought one out onto the counter, and set it beside the plastic juice jug. By feeling the lid, Hope could tell it was open. She lined the jug with her glass while using the tip of her index finger to feel when the liquid reached the top.

As she raised the glass to her lips, Hope couldn't help but feel a sense of satisfaction that she'd been able to do something on her own. After a couple of swallows of the sweet juice, she set it back down onto the counter and said, "Booyah. That's what I'm talking about."

It had taken three days of practice to do that, so she added a little dance to go along with her statement. She understood this was a minor accomplishment to others, but it proved she could learn to do things another way and survive.

Clapping came from the front door, but it didn't startle Hope. She'd scented Sarah before she'd even entered her home.

"That's wonderful, Hope," Sarah congratulated. By her footsteps she was moving forward to sit on the couch.

"Thank you. I've been trying to get the basics down." It hadn't been easy.

Hope picked up her glass of juice and began counting paces on her way to the couch. The children had been good about not leaving their toys and belongings lying out on the floor for her to trip over. Gareth had taken to sleeping on the couch to be available if she or the children needed anything.

She still couldn't figure him out. He'd refused to come over for breakfast when she'd been trying to make amends for sending him away, having Sarah return with the plates instead. However, now he'd pretty much moved in. Was it pity? She didn't want to be pitied by anyone.

When her fingertips touched the arm of the couch, Hope made her way along the front until she could sense Sarah was only a couple feet away and sat down.

"You're getting around better every day, Hope. I knew you would." There was no pity in her tone. Just simple facts and congratulations. Sarah had become a very dear friend to Hope, and throughout these latest events, she'd become her cheerleader.

"I wish I had your optimism," Hope said. "Tell me the truth, is what I'm wearing even matching?" Sarah broke out into a fit of laughter. "Don't laugh. I have a male tiger-shifter and two children under seven picking out my clothing every morning." Hope tried to keep a straight face, but soon she found herself laughing along with Sarah. "I could be wearing a purple polka dot shirt with orange pants for all I know."

Other than with the children, this was the first time she'd laughed since losing her sight, and it lifted her spirits. Sarah was a rare white hyena who didn't follow other hyena-shifters who worked for the human hunters and now the demons. She had great power, and it honestly surprised Hope that she wasn't a reincarnated goddess along with Raz, Rose, and Zahra. However, Sarah didn't have the markings indicative of the five original warrior goddesses.

Raz had black filigree tattoos covering her body. Rose had white, and Zahra had the Eyes of Ra on both of her palms. These markings typically lit up when the three used their powers, which ranged from telekinesis, mind-reading, teleportation, freezing and capturing demons, bringing the dead back to life, using voice to influence others, increasing physical size in shifted form. And many other capabilities Hope knew nothing about.

Sarah could manipulate metal and other matter to her will, evidenced by her saving their new homes from a destroyed ventilation system, rebuilding engines, or tearing machines they'd taken from the demons apart to see inside, which was coming in handy now the demons had created a few new toys designed to harm shifters. One was a collar that forced the wearer to do what they were told, and another was a machine they'd recovered that could suck the very life out of a shifter and transfer it into a Collector Demon. This allowed them to remain inside the same host body instead of regularly switching as had always been the way. It also gave them the ability to accomplish much more since they no longer had to race against time while their human shell decomposed around them.

Once Sarah got herself back under control, she said, "You look fine. Trust me. I wouldn't let you walk around in anything you'd be embarrassed about. In truth, Gareth has already asked my opinion on his choices. He wanted to make sure you dressed like your normal self."

"He did? Why would he care?" The comment came out without thinking and she hated sounding ungrateful.

"Okay, I know you're blind, but you are not an imbecile," Sarah huffed.

"Gee, thanks." Leave it to her closest friend to not change her candor no matter Hope's condition.

"That man is head over heels for you, my bear friend."

"He loves the children, and you made him swear to watch over us. That is not head over heels love. That's being a decent shifter and a man of his word."

"Okay, imbecile is back on the table."

"Hey."

"Well, if you're going to act like one, I'm going to call you on it. His actions have nothing to do with an oath to me, and what's wrong with Gareth loving the children and taking care of them, exactly?" Sarah asked.

"He's doing all this for me out of pity." Though Hope hated knowing she had allowed herself to care deeply for him and, worst of all, depend on him.

"How do you figure?" Sarah's voice sounded high-pitched and honestly confused.

"When I was tricked into having a physical, I told him I had to think and to go away. He played with the children for three days but didn't stop for a second to look or talk to me. When I sent him an apology dinner and asked him to come over for breakfast, he sent you with the empty plates. It wasn't until I woke up in the infirmary he started talking to me again. So, yeah, pity." Hope couldn't stop her hands from shaking with emotion. She hadn't been so hurt in a long time.

Silence. Now that she couldn't see Sarah's expression, Hope had difficulty judging emotion when faced with dead air. Despite feeling confused, she was getting through their clan blood bond, but Hope was unsure why her friend had gone silent.

"Um, Sarah? Can we skip over the silence? It's freaking me out when I can't see you."

"Oh, shit, sorry," Sarah said as she snapped out of whatever she'd been doing. "You honestly thought Gareth had given you a brush off that morning you had your attack."

"What was I supposed to think. You were there with the plates, not him." Facts.

"Oh, sweetheart, that's not what happened." Gareth's voice came from somewhere near the doorway. "I was the one who was in the wrong in that entire situation."

Hope had to admit she'd been so engrossed in their conversation she hadn't sensed him nearing before he was within earshot, and now she didn't know what to do. This wasn't the conversation she wanted or planned to have, ever.

"I'll go watch the children while the two of you talk," Sarah said, and left them alone.

Hope sensed Gareth coming closer until he was sitting beside her on the couch. Hope was scrambling for something to say, but now she seemed to have lost her voice. *Great.*

He slowly took hold of her fidgeting hands and said, "I was on my way here that morning when Ben asked me to give him a hand, so I handed the tray to Sarah. I wasn't snubbing your invitation, and I wasn't staying away from you because of anything you did."

"Then why?" She'd been there, and it sure as hell felt like she was being ignored.

"Because I'd acted like an idiot, a juvenile tiger having a temper tantrum. You deserved to be pissed at what we did. It was underhanded, and no way to build trust between us. I shouldn't have gone along with it."

"It's likely the only way to get Jewel and me in the same room," Hope admitted. "There was no way I would have gone to see her."

"Why?" Gareth asked. "You were in such pain it was killing me to watch."

Hope knew she had to be truthful before everything came to a head. "I was afraid I'd be found unfit to take care of the children any longer. That Jenny and Matthew would be taken away to be raised by another shifter."

Chapter Five

Gareth looked at Hope in a new light. How had he been so wrong? Instead of being stubborn or controlling, she was doing everything in her power to hold onto the children. He should have known; Hope's heart and head were always focused on Jenny and Matthew.

"I'm so sorry," he said. "I should've understood your motivation. You've been selfless throughout your life. I don't know why would that change now."

"I'm not a pushover," she growled. She hated being considered weaker than the rest because she chose kindness and understanding.

"That's not what selfless means," Gareth explained.

"According to my older brother, it was," Hope stated.

"Brother?" He'd wondered about her family, considering he'd never seen them around. "Does he live here in the bunker?" 'Cause he'd set him straight about Hope being weak.

She looked away before answering. "No. He and my parents were killed by human hunters a long time ago."

Shit.

"I'm sorry. I didn't mean to bring up anything painful." He never wanted to cause her pain.

She turned around to face him. "I know you would never intentionally cause me pain. I trust you."

Gareth felt his heart speeding up with her admission of trust in him. That was what he'd wanted from the beginning. Now he had it, he would never do anything to break it.

"Thank you, that means the world to me." Gareth allowed his feelings for her to flow through their private link. This was the first time either of them had used it, and he was concerned he'd overstepped his bounds.

He watched Hope's face run through emotions from her brow-raising surprise to squinting confusion and thankfully on to the contented smile of happiness. She hadn't opened her side of the link, and he hadn't expected such a cautious woman to do that. However, Hope now knew his true feelings and hadn't sent him packing. He'd take that as a win.

Hope slid the few feet over on the couch and used her hands to determine his position before wrapping her arms around his neck and pulling him close. "Thank you, Gareth, for understanding me. I care about you so much, but I can't think of my needs right now. I must give the children all my attention while figuring out how to live if this blindness is permanent. I wouldn't be able to give you what you deserve."

"You let me worry about what I deserve. I'm not going anywhere; I understand the children's needs must always come first and wholeheartedly agree. I care about all three of you."

Hope held him tighter, and even though he couldn't see her face, Gareth knew there were tears in her eyes. This strong she-bear allowed herself to show what she considered a weakness in front of him. No words of love could ever compare.

***

Hope could feel something deep inside of her let go, and the flood gates opened, freeing emotions she'd stamped down decades ago, resurfacing as sharply. Gareth hadn't run. Instead, he'd tightened his hold. This allowed her to grieve in a way she'd never done before. Even after her family was taken, Hope had shown no weakness. Through it all, Gareth held her silently, her rock through the storm of emotions. Guilt from having been the only one in her family to survive the attack, fear of being left alone, unimaginable pain from her family's death, and the final insult, the loss of her family home and all the daily reminders of her family once the demons began taking over.

When Hope felt able to pull herself together, she realized two things. First, she now had her head on Gareth's chest, and they were both leaning back against the couch cushions. Second, the apartment door was shut, and they were alone.

"The children?" Hope said as she lifted her head.

"Don't worry, they are well taken care of," Gareth said while rubbing his hand up and down her back in a soothing motion. "Sarah and Joseph are with them. They are watching a movie and munching on popcorn. Happy and content."

Hope felt bad that she was a little annoyed no one had told her through the communal link. After all, it was obvious they had contacted Gareth.

"You deserved a moment for yourself, Hope," Gareth answered.

"How did you know what I was thinking? I wasn't sharing it through the link."

"I could sense your concern. The rest I figured out because I'm beginning to understand you."

Had anyone ever known her well enough to pick up on her cues so easily and decipher them without effort?

Knowing the children were safe and happy, Hope allowed herself to lay her head back onto Gareth's broad chest and relax. The strong beat of his heart lulled her into a sense of safety and security as she sorted through her memories.

"My brother wasn't a jerk." She didn't want Gareth to think that. "He was worried people would take advantage of me. Shifter and human alike."

"He was protective of you. I can understand that and respect it. How old were you when they died?" Gareth asked.

"Twenty-two. Decades ago, but somedays it feels like only days have passed. I was there when it happened. When the human-hunters came for us." She didn't like that her voice shook but didn't try to curate her emotions in front of Gareth. If this had a chance of working, they both needed to be open and honest.

Gareth's hold strengthened around her, and she felt his fear through their link. He'd opened his link fully to her, but Hope was still unsure, mainly due to her recent change. After all, he was a tiger-shifter in his prime. What could she, a blind bear-shifter with two human children, ever have to offer him? Of course, her worry over losing her new family drove her to think as soon as he figured that out, Gareth would be gone.

"We were off for a fun day by one of the lakes on clan property, far away from any borders. It should have been safe. I'd even baked cupcakes for the trip." The fact seemed so trivial now. Did they even eat them? "My family wasn't the only one at the lake that day. Other bear families were out enjoying the warm day. Children were running through the trees and laughing in both their shifted and unshifted forms. It was perfect. My brother was off swimming in the lake in bear form while mom and dad were visiting another family. I was relaxing back against a tree reading my book when the first gunshots rang out behind me."

Hope could still recall them ricocheting off the oak tree she hid behind.

"It lasted less than a minute before fellow bears took down the hunters, but the results of their attack were horrific." A shiver raced down her spine. "When I came out of hiding, there were shifter bodies in both forms laying on the ground as far as I could see. Some were still alive and healing, while others would never rise again. I found my parents first. My dad's body was covering my mom's, attempting to protect her, but they'd been too close to the location where the hunters came out of the forest. I frantically searched for my brother, and when I found him, he was in much the same position as my dad, only the child he'd protected with his own life survived."

Hope could feel more tears trailing down her cheeks but didn't care. She was safe here with Gareth. His arms never weakened, holding her tight, being exactly who and what she needed at that moment. For that respite, she knew she'd never be able to repay him.

"You were left alone," Gareth said.

"Yes, but it wasn't because Alpha Mason and Beta Riker hadn't tried to change that. They invited me to live inside the clan house full-time, and my fellow clan members stood by my side, offering anything they could do to help. In the end, I decided to stay in my family's home. It was where I could still sense them even if I couldn't touch them anymore."

"Is that why you created the exterior of your home here to look like your old home?"

"Yes." Hope wasn't surprised Gareth knew that. He was an intelligent tiger and much more observant than she'd given him credit for.

"And the day I walked into your life, you were losing your home once again."

"Yes, only this time it was the new home I'd made with the children."

Gareth rubbed the top of her head with his jaw. "Why did the triads choose you to foster the children?"

"They didn't. I approached the triads after the children were rescued. They were all alone, and so was I. So, I figured we could join forces and make it through this together." Felt right at the time, and still did.

In truth, the children gave Hope more than anything she could give them. They'd given her a family and a reason to keep fighting. She no longer felt alone in the world among the hundreds of members of the clan. Jenny and Matthew's unconditional love was what drove her to make sure they were healthy and happy, and she'd fight to the death to keep it that way.

"And you selflessly dedicated your life to raising two human children even after human hunters took your family away. Of all shifters that could hold a grudge against humans, you are certainly more entitled than most. Being this way makes you strong, not weak. You saw past the fact that they were human and simply saw their need. I respect your strength of character."

Hope hadn't ever considered the events that way. She'd seen the need of the two frightened children and filled it. She'd been fulfilling needs most of her life. When Sarah had first been rescued, she'd stayed in her white hyena form, so Hope gathered a selection of soft fabrics, ever mindful of her friend's scars, and made clothing for her. She'd also visited the storage area to collect a pair of shoes and jeans for Sarah. Days later, the nervous white hyena-shifter came out of hiding in her human form for the first time dressed in Hope's clothing.

The storage area was on the lower levels and contained items the teams would bring back from the surface. Search parties would teleport to the surface with a goddesses' help, and if they came across anything useful, they'd try to bring it back. On occasion, they'd run into a derelict department store and bring racks of clothing back along with fabrics, canned and freeze-dried foods, furniture, toys for the children, DVDs to add to their offered selections, electronics, rechargeable batteries, and so much more.

It wasn't only new items available in the storage area. The bunkers had a healthy reuse policy. All the clothing that Jenny and Matthew grew out of was cleaned, repaired, and hung in the same area for another family to use. There was a team created specially to organize the entire place. As they grew and their interests changed, she and the children would return a toy and search out a new one.

Anything that was worn down and could no longer serve its purpose was recycled. Worn-out clothing could be used as rags down on the farm level.

Gareth rubbed her back with soothing circles, and Sarah didn't know whether it was all the changes or the tender moment, but she'd never wanted to kiss a man more in her life. She thought about it as she always did, analyzing if it would be the right move when it hit her; this was life. She couldn't calculate risk and reward, safety and future when it came to life and love. With renewed purpose, she raised her head, and even though she couldn't see all his love shining back at her, she could feel it. The time for caution was over, and with it all her fears of allowing the handsome tiger-shifter into her life.

"I want to kiss you," she stated. "But I'm not sure where your lips are."

Gareth's quick intake of breath let her know she wasn't the only one with that idea. "I'd love to kiss you."

Hope felt his large hand cup the side of her face and could sense him moving closer. When their lips met for the first time, Hope wasn't prepared for the emotions that touch caused. Excitement, need, and a rush of happiness raced through her body as their kiss deepened. Tongues explored at a leisurely pace as Hope held tightly onto Gareth. The kiss slowed. Both were breathing heavy, and he pulled her closer.

"If you ever want to do that again, you just let me know," Gareth said, his voice deeper than before.

Hope couldn't help but laugh softly. "I'll make sure of it."

As she relaxed even further, Hope's senses picked up something else in the room with them. In the next moment, a red shadow floated across the blackness of her vision. At first, she thought her eyes weren't to be trusted, but then it happened again. She tensed, and Gareth's demeanor changed immediately.

"What is it?" He asked, his grip tightening.

Hope raised her head and sat straight up. She could feel the hairs on her arms raising as alarm bells sounded in some part of her that she'd never felt before. It wasn't coming from her bear and felt substantially stronger.

"Do you see it?" she asked Gareth as the vapor cloud-like fog moved from one part of the living room to another. Could it be her vision screwing up further?

Gareth was on full alert beside her. "Where is it?"

"In the corner. It's a shadowy red shape floating near the ceiling."

"I don't see anything, Hope. Could it be your vision coming back?"

"This doesn't feel right to me. There's something there. I can feel it."

"I believe you. The only other shadowy thing I know of is a Collector Demon, but they're black, and we have safeguards stopping them from getting into the bunker system. I can't sense anything other than you in this room."

The shape flashed across the room as if searching for something, zigzagging its way across the ceiling and began emitting beeps and small squealing noises near the children's bedroom door. Hope suddenly realized the shape was looking for the children. "It's not supposed to be here. Not near the children." Hope's body began heating.

"Do you think it's a demon? How could one of them get down here with all the protections and goddess enchantments?"

Hope didn't answer, but the closer the shadow came to her children's bedroom door, the angrier she became. Her bear was pushing for freedom to deal with the intruder, but one thought stopped her from releasing it. What if it wasn't real and only a figment of her messed-up sight. She wished she had the same faith in herself Gareth had.

Hope moved closer to the red vapor as it hovered above her. The fog moved in waves. Sometimes it was opaque, while others it was nearly transparent. There was something in there, and it didn't feel right. Hope tried sharing what she was seeing with the clan and pack when suddenly two shining eyes flashed while looking directly at her. Demon.

Hope's body lit up like it was on fire as what felt like lightning bolts pulsed across her skin, quickly replaced by dark fur. Her bear was done with possible explanations, and it was time for the creature to leave. She shot upwards, stretching her now glowing claws out and raking them through the shadow. How could she see her claws now?

The creature hissed its anger, but nothing would stop Hope from protecting her family. Using the kitchen counter as a springboard the she-bear launched herself at the uninvited visitor taking the overhead lighting crashing down with her. The red shadow darted from side to side but couldn't seem to get past the living room and kitchen area. When she dug her claws into the vapor again, she could feel them sinking into something, and blood began to flow. Or at least that's what Hope thought it might be because her paws were now wet.

She could sense Gareth had shifted into his tiger to back her up even though he couldn't see the creature himself. It meant the world to Hope. She dug her claws in even deeper now that she had the demon until a wailing screech was followed by a loud crunch. The creature seemed to solidify before her messed up eyes before falling limp from her claws and onto the ground.

Hope's shock had her arms flailed out to her sides banging her hands off broken pieces of wood. The more she felt around, she realized the fight had destroyed her kitchen and living room, but also the outline of the destruction was visible to her.

Wait, the longer she stared at items around her the more she could see, well, partially. Mainly the outline of things like an overexposed picture, but she'd take it. Her bear picked the dead creature up and carried it out of their home for all to see now it was dead and appeared visible. Meaning it had the ability to cloak itself. Scary.

"What is it?" Marie asked. Hope was happy to have an outline to look at when someone was talking. You never notice how important things are until you lose them. "You're looking straight at me. Can you see me again?"

"Only the outline of things, but I'll take it," she replied through the link as she was still in her bear form.

"I couldn't see what you were fighting, but the image you sent through the link came through loud and clear," Ben said. His grizzly's canines slightly muffled his voice as he 'd partially shifted. "Now that it's dead we all can see it plain as day."

Hope noticed that Sarah, Jenny, and Matthew were nowhere in sight. *"Where are my children?"* she asked through her clan link to the people present in the restricted area.

"Safe with Sarah in our bedroom," Joseph answered. "When you sent us that warning, we went into lockdown."

"Thank you."

"Don't the Collector Demons turn to dust when they are killed?" Joan asked from her position slightly behind her son Ben. The grizzly bear-shifter still wasn't one-hundred percent sure of the clan yet, considering she'd been banished by her own when she had a child with a human.

"Yes, they do," Marie answered with a growl. "This is not a Collector Demon."

Hope looked over at Sarah and Joseph's door to find the outline of Sarah's sister, the small white hyena they'd recently saved from the demons, standing guard in front of the door. The hyena was protecting Hope's children inside. Even though she had been too frightened to come out earlier, she put her fear aside for them. Hope prayed the small shifter could feel the thanks she was sending her way for her show of bravery. When the white hyena looked directly at her and nodded her head, Hope had her answer.

"No, it is not," Raz's voice broke through the gathered crowd, which parted to allow the alpha triads, Zahra, and John, though.

Hope looked down at the faded red form oozing black liquid from the damage she had committed. *"What is it, Raz?"*

"I've been researching through all the known records of the last war and found a reference to red beings. The scholars referred to them as Deshr, the word for red, the color of chaos and disorder," Raz explained briefly. "I'll have to dig deeper for more details."

"Do we know what its purpose is?" Rose asked as she examined the creature. "We need to get this back to the lab to take it apart. Find out what makes it tick."

"Yeah, like why Hope was able to grab onto a solid form when the fog showed none in the vision she shared with us," Mason said as more Warriors filled in.

"Can they inhabit a human host?" General John, Zahra's mate, asked.

"How did they get through our safeguards," Zahra asked. *"We'd worked days on them."*

"It was looking for my children," Hope said bluntly. *"I could sense that."*

A spike of fear shot through those in the restricted area.

"Okay, this is what we're going to do," Alpha Matriarch Raz commanded. "First, we take this thing to the lab and begin dissecting it. Second, we goddesses will reinforce our safeguards even further in hopes of stopping them from entering or at least slowing them down. Until we have an idea what's going on, Hope, you need to stay close to Jenny and Matthew in case there are more."

"Do you think there is any threat to the shifter children?" Hope asked. The last thing she wanted was for any of the little ones to be targeted.

"You said you could sense its presence, right?" Xander mentioned.

"Yes. I could feel something was off before it appeared."

"Do you think you could try expanding your range to cover the bunkers until we figure this out?" Xander continued.

"I can try," she said. *"I can't promise anything because this is all new to me, but I swear to give it all I have."*

"Do your best, and if you sense something similar, contact me immediately so I can teleport you to wherever you sense it in the bunker system in case it's another Deshr," Raz commanded.

"Why would you want to take me there?" Hope asked.

"Because at the moment, you, Hope, are the only shifter capable of seeing them and the power to reform the demon so it can be injured," Raz explained.

"Right." Hope was still shaken up after the attack. Her brain was running in a million directions. Then she keyed in on one inescapable fact. *"Was this why my vision was taken from me? So that I could see the invisible threat."*

Rose, the bear clan, and Hope's Alpha Matriarch looked at her in thought. "Perhaps. The Gods don't typically ask permission before resurrecting a goddess."

Hope shifted back to human form so quickly she made herself dizzy. "Goddess? I'm no goddess."

Gareth began raising his fingers as he spoke. "You have an amazing freaky ability to sense and kill an invisible threat. You have lightning bolts flowing across your skin, much like Raz's filigree and the Eye of Ra on the other goddesses. Sounds about right, Goddess Hope."

"Don't you start," Hope growled. "If I were truly a goddess, wouldn't I have more powers than that?"

"You don't know all your abilities yet. More could appear."

Hope didn't want to get into this. She looked down to find she was covered in remnants of the creature. "I'm going to have a shower and then go hug my children." Needing space, Hope turned around and walked back into her home. With her new overprocessed vision, she could easily avoid the splintered couch, smashed glass, and shredded drywall on her way to the bathroom. She needed a minute to wrap the events of the day around her mind.

Could the Gods have taken her sight so she could see these Deshr? Was she one of the five warrior goddesses reincarnating to lead the fight against the demons? Hell, she could barely lead herself to the shower. Who in their right mind would ever follow her?

Chapter Six

"There has to be an answer in here somewhere," Marian, Raz's mother-in-law, growled as she closed another tome from the Ancients. Some pieces were still preserved on their original papyrus. "There has to be more information on these Deshr Demons."

Raz looked up from the Middle Kingdom's ancient hieroglyphs to watch Marian throwing up her arms in defeat. Marian, a fellow mage just like herself, had taught Raz so much since they'd first met years ago.

"I agree. This is getting us nowhere," Raz huffed and rubbed her sore eyes. "Between the two of us, we should be able to come up with something to aid in this situation."

Marian got a faraway look on her face as Raz wracked her brain for a spell or summoning to help them find the information they drastically needed. With their combined strength and skill, it shouldn't be impossible. She looked over the scrolls, tablets, artifacts, and books collected for safekeeping inside the vault. She wondered if they were doing enough to preserve not only shifter history but human as well. Perhaps she'd discuss this with her mates as well as the possibility of sending a rescue team to a couple of large archives around the world, starting with London's Archaeological Archive and on to the Vatican City's secret archives.

"I've got it," Marian shouted, scaring Raz back to the here and now.

"What?'

"The spell I believe will give us a leg up on this search. I'll need to borrow some of your power to accomplish this."

"Of course, take what you need," Raz said while holding out her hand.

"Always ready to help others. My sons are fortunate to have been blessed with you as their mate," Marian said and took hold of her offered hand.

Raz could instantly feel the power exchange between them, and her goddess filigree markings began heating up all over her body. Marian began chanting in Old Egyptian, but Raz could only make out a few words from her lessons. Sight, red, demon, and children were a few she understood, confirming she needed to increase her studies.

The rhythm seemed to fill the room as waves of invisible power crashed and flowed around them, slamming the open door shut. Voices joined in even though they were still standing alone, the hum joining together until there was nothing else. No world beyond this room existed as golden symbols rose into the air above the books and artifacts laying out shifter history. An Ankh – life - resembling a cross but with a loop for the top piece; Scarab, - immortality, resurrection – rebirth; and the Udjat Eye – protection, royal power, good health – better known as the symbol for the Eye of Horus. All three glowed like the sun itself, forcing Raz to close her eyes.

The voices raised into a crescendo before pouring down over the contents of the room, then silence. Raz opened her eyes to find Marian still standing beside her.

"Is it over?" Raz asked.

Marian took a few steps forward and looked down at the items they'd been searching in for answers. "Come see for yourself, daughter."

Raz went to stand beside her, and when she looked at the writings and drawings, she'd been deciphering they'd changed. There were references to the red demon and those with the power to stop them. As she continued to read, Raz began to panic. According to this, the Deshr demons were attracted to children or, more specifically, their innocence. She needed her daughter in her arms, and that had to happen now.

"Be right back," Raz said before teleporting herself to their private area of the bunker to find Asta safe in Xander's arms.

The moment Xander sensed her presence, he turned to face her. "Mate, what is it? Are you okay?"

Raz couldn't help but hold out her arms for Asta to climb into. She'd never been this scared before. Even when she was being held at that sick safari all those years, she'd never been terrified. Xander came over and wrapped them both in his strong arms as Axel came bursting through the doors.

"Mate, I could sense your distress. What's wrong?" Axel asked as he joined their little huddle.

"I'm sorry for scaring both of you, but your mother and I came across information on the Deshr, and it's worse than I could have ever imagined. Hope was right; the red demons are coming for our children. They hunt out their innocence."

Raz buried her face in her daughter's silky hair, and even though she was still a toddler, Asta sensed their stress and held on tight. This wasn't the world she wanted for her child or any of the children in this bunker. Then it struck her if these demons could hunt down innocence, any children still above ground would be at grave risk.

"We have to protect the children," Raz declared.

"And Hope as it turns out," Marian's voice shocked her for the second time today.

"Hope?" Raz asked.

"Yes. It appears I have discovered which goddess has been reincarnated inside of our Hope, and you're never going to believe me."

***

"The Egyptian goddess, Isis," Marian stated.

"The Goddess of Motherhood, protector of women and children, to be exact," Raz clarified.

"You're trying to tell me I'm Isis?" Hope asked in shock.

"No. What I'm saying is that she has bestowed her powers onto you," Marian clarified.

"You must have done something special to garner the goddess's favor," Raz said almost clapping in happiness.

"Making me a goddess?" Hope didn't feel well.

"Yes," Marian declared.

Hope stared back at everyone gathered. Everything in the restricted area's large, airy courtyard seemed frozen in time waiting on her response. From the small geometric-shaped bushes scattered throughout to Archie and the pillow-puppy, all waited on her. Hope's mouth opened and closed a few times like a fish, but no words came out. Both triads, Zahra and John, Gareth, Jenny and Matthew, Marie, Ben, Joan, Sarah, her sister, and Joseph, seemed to be in stunned silence as well. This couldn't be happening. "Of all people, why me?" This didn't make sense. There were those who could do so much more with this power.

"I happen to believe Isis has chosen wisely," Zahra said.

Hope couldn't help but smile at her friend's confidence in her. Considering the she-wolf was one of the Eyes of Ra, it carried some weight.

"You have to admit, you are the consummate mother figure. You care for others before yourself, and you ensure that everyone has what they need most when they need it," Sarah agreed.

"Protective isn't a strong enough word to describe you, Hope, when confronted with any threat," Ben chimed in.

"And being an all-around kind and decent person," Marie said. "Helps."

Hope was speechless at her friends' words. Was this what they genuinely thought of her?

"Damn straight it is," Gareth's voice came along their private link full of pride.

"How do you keep reading my thoughts? I didn't send that over the link," Hope asked. "You did it before in the infirmary."

"Sweetheart, I mentioned previously I understand how you think, and it's quite easy to read your emotions on your face. Just now you looked around at us in shock and it wasn't hard to put two and two together that you didn't know how everyone saw you."

She looked in the tiger-shifters eyes, unable to see the color only the outlines but knowing it didn't matter she couldn't see the green shade anymore if this gift helped her protect children. "Thank you."

"So, how did the goddess become involved in the first war?" Joseph asked.

"As far as we can tell, the goddess showed up after the first Deshr appeared. The red demons hunted children from both the human and shifter populations. They couldn't possess a child much like their Collector Demons cousins, but they can influence the child's thoughts," Raz explained.

"Influence?" Hope asked. "What kind of influence?"

"Yes. These demons can manipulate their thoughts and memories. Often resulting in the child coming out of hiding to reveal themselves to the collectors, or to pick up arms against their own family and friends," Marian growled as she spoke, obviously angered by the threat.

"How old does the child have to become before they are immune to the Deshr's influence?" Gareth asked.

"The clearest mention we could uncover stated the end of puberty," Raz explained.

"So, sixteen to eighteen years old depending on the child," Mason stated in disbelief. "We need to inform all shifter colonies immediately."

"How many Deshr are there?" Hope asked.

"There isn't a known number recorded but by the accounts, there seemed to be more than the one you killed, Hope," Raz answered, looking about as bleak as Hope felt.

Jewel had joined their group and appeared to be lost in thought.

"Jewel, are you okay?" Hope asked.

The doctor looked up and said, "I don't know. I've been having an uptick in children being seen in the infirmary these past couple weeks. Do you think this had something to do with the Deshrs?"

"We'll have to look into each case to make sure," Rose announced. "Maybe this is why you've been having headaches for a while now, Hope."

Seconds later, something changed. The hair on Hope's arms stood on end, a notable high-pitched squeal sounded, and Sarah's sister, still in her hyena form, came rushing out of her apartment door where she'd been listening, getting everyone's attention. Could there be two of them who'd received this gift? More help to protect the children was just what she needed and desperately prayed it was true.

"I feel it again, and I believe so does our new friend." The typically shy hyena had raced to Hope's side and began pawing her leg. "Yes, we sense another one in the bunkers."

"Where? Show me," Raz growled as she held out her hand so that she could share the image and teleport them where the creature was hunting a child.

Hope looked down at Jenny and Matthew, safe beside Gareth. "I'll be right back, sweethearts."

She dug her hand into the hyena's fur and grabbed Raz's hand. The world swirled around her as she held on tight, but within seconds her new adjusted sight cleared enough to discover the three of them were in a living room. Hope and the hyena took off for the hallway, and halfway down, she noticed the drops of blood on the carpeting. *Shit.* Were they too late?

When they charged into the first bedroom, Hope saw a sight she never wanted to be repeated. A male and female wolf-shifter were kneeling on the floor. The male had knife wounds on his arms, but they appeared to be superficial. The real concern was the boy huddled in the corner, holding a knife to his own throat. He looked to Hope to be at most eleven years old.

Hope scanned the room and found the red Deshr along the wall on the far side of the bed. It was influencing the boy into harming his parents and now taking his own life. The parents were begging for him to lower the knife, but the boy's face remained blank.

"To hell with that, you red asshole," Hope growled before launching herself at the Deshr with the white hyena by her side. She shifted her hands into paws and flashed her claws as her body heated up, and lightning bolts shot across not only her skin but the hyena's as well.

The creature hissed as Hope's claws sliced through the foggy mist. The second her hand was out of the way her hyena companion charged forward and dug her sharp canines into the invisible Deshr taking the creature to the ground. Hope followed them down as the shape solidified. Even with her overprocessed black and white sight, Hope could make out the red of the Deshr and perhaps was beginning to understand the change in her sight. Hope could pick up on the demons without effort with this vision, and she couldn't help but wonder how the hyena saw things.

With a fatal blow delivered by the hyena, the Deshr screeched its last, leaving only the noise of their heavy breathing from the exertion. The fight may not have been long, but it took a wallop out of Hope each time. She hoped with any luck she'd gain some stamina if this was to become a frequent event.

"What the hell are a bear and filthy hyena doing in our home? What's that thing on the floor?" The male wolf growled from across the room. Behind him, the boy was now wrapped in the she-wolf's arms, safe, knife nowhere to be seen. Hope thought perhaps the small hyena with the power over all material had something to do with its disappearance.

Raz was quick to step in. "That thing on the floor is a Deshr demon, and those two are here saving your son's life. Show some respect."

The wolf-shifter fell to his knees in front of Goddess Raz the moment he saw her.

Hope didn't want to stick around for the discussion. She longed to be home with her children and damned if it didn't happen. She'd been thinking about their home, and now she was standing in the center of her living room, and if her new eyesight wasn't messing with her, the little white hyena was back in her apartment window.

Slowly Hope began moving different parts of her body, ensuring that all of her was indeed back in her home. "Did I just teleport?"

"Yes, you did," Rose said from the open doorway.

"Whoa, these powers are becoming stronger, and I'm positive the Goddess Isis has also blessed our new hyena friend," Hope declared.

"We noticed that as well. Raz reports that the boy is well with no memory of the event and that she's healed the father's wounds," Rose explained.

"That's good," Hope said as she noticed she was free of any evidence of the fight, such as blood or even damaged clothing and that there was a slight sparkle to her skin. Had her skin changed? "Am I shining?"

"Your lightning bolts have become a permanent part of your body," Rose confirmed. "Much like the white filigree I have, the black of Raz's, and the Eyes of Ra on Zahra's hands. They declare your status as goddess."

"The children have already been put through enough change without this," Hope huffed as she raised her shiny arms high.

"Wow." A small voice said from behind Rose. "You're a superhero." Gareth and the children walked in from the courtyard.

Hope went to her knees and opened her arms for Matthew. Her little boy had spoken his first words, and it was to tell Hope she was a superhero. How had she ever gotten this lucky with her own little family? Which now included a bear, two human children, and a tiger-shifter?

"You sparkle like a fairy," Jenny said as she joined in on the hug.

Gareth stood back, and Rose had left them alone. Without an ounce of hesitation, Hope opened her left arm and motioned towards the big tiger. No words were needed as he went to his knees to join the three of them.

This, right here, was family.

Chapter Seven

They're looking at me. Elena didn't like that, but who could blame them? She was glowing like a light bulb, after all. Was there a way to turn this shit off? Her sister, Sarah, was headed in her direction, and she knew what she wanted to talk about, but Elena wasn't sure she was ready for that. She hadn't even tried to initiate their sisterly link since their reunion. No one wanted to see inside her head, she worried memories might spill over into the link. However, she'd chosen her name as she didn't have one before she was stolen and desperately wanted to share it with Sarah. It had been their mother's name; Elena.

An internal door attached their apartments, and thankfully Sarah decided to knock on that door instead of the front door. It felt more personal somehow. Of course, Sarah was her sister, and she loved her, but they'd been apart for many years, and both had changed. When the rescue teams from the bunker initially saved her from her demon captors, it was only by scent Elena recognized her sister.

Elena had been held alone for so long that groups of people made her nervous, but she'd had to protect those children when the warning bells went off inside her head. Now she had the same markings as the bear-shifter, but there was no way in hell she was a goddess like Hope. Elena knew that all the good was drained out of her long ago by the Collector Demons. They'd been bent on controlling her powers, leaving her feeling like a shell of a being.

Not goddess material.

The knock made her jump even though she'd expected it. Sarah opened the door and popped her head inside.

"Sis, can we talk?" Sarah looked worried, and Elena didn't want to cause her to feel that way.

Elena saw no way out of it, so she nodded her hyena's head, and stepped back a safe distance. How long would it take her to get over her fear of everyone? She could see the pain it caused her sister but was powerless to stop those ingrained reactions.

Sarah shut the door behind her and came to sit on the floor a few feet away from Elena. "Are you hurt?" Her concern was evident.

Of course, she'd come to check if Elena was hurt in all of this. Sarah was a loving and caring sister, which made her decision a bit easier about reopening their link, at least partway. She still couldn't risk her memories reaching Sarah.

"I can have Jewel come take a look at you," Sarah offered as she slowly reached for Elena's paw. "I'd be right here by your side the entire time, sister."

"Elena," she said through their bonded link. Her voice sounded odd to her even though it was only by thought; then again, she'd been silent for decades. She could only imagine her human form's voice being much the same after years of disuse. *"I chose Elena for my name."*

"Our mother's name," Sarah said while running her fingers through Elena's fur. "It's beautiful." Tears began flooding Sarah's eyes as Elena closed the distance between them and laid her hyena's head on her sister's arm. She didn't want to make her cry.

"I missed you so much," Elena said as their link grew stronger now that it was back in use. However, she was cautious not to show too much. Sarah didn't need any additional nightmares.

Sarah wrapped her arms around Elena and gave her a strong hug. "I don't want us to be apart ever again."

"Neither do I," Elena said, and she had an idea. *"Could you close the drapes and lock the doors, please."* In for a penny, in for a pound as their mom used to say.

Sarah stood and did as she had asked. Now came the scary part. There was more than one reason why Elena hadn't shifted in the months that she'd been here in the bunkers. Of course, safety, even though no one had threatened her, but also fear that she wouldn't be able to bring on the shift. Considering she hadn't been in her human form since the day they were kidnapped as children, to say she was out of practice was an understatement.

"I haven't done this in a while," Elena admitted. *"Not sure I remember how."* She'd been young the last time, and certain memories had faded. *"And honestly, I didn't go out of my way to remember considering I never intended to shift again."*

Sarah got onto her hands and knees and shifted seamlessly into her white hyena, allowing her dress to slide to the floor at the change in her size. The sisters had always been considered odd due to their white fur and pale skin. Most hyenas' furs were dark in color, with browns and blacks. They'd been considered weak because they would not follow the other hyenas in tracking other shifters for their human hunter masters. Now Collector Demons ran the show, and the hunters and hyenas worked for them.

"I will walk you through it. We'll be side by side, and if you need to stop at any time, we will," Sarah reassured, making Elena a little less stressed. *"It might take a few tries. We can practice as many times as you'd like,"*

"Thank you, Sarah. You always had a knack for making things easier on me." Though Elena could only remember bits and pieces of her past, she was confident of that one memory.

"Because I love you. You're my sister."

Elena rubbed the side of her hyena body against her sister's and said, *"I love you too. You were always the best to me."*

Sarah rubbed her muzzle along Elena's side. *"Ready?"*

Elena stood straight and focused on Sarah. *"As I'll ever be."* She could do this. Right?

"You know how to do it. It's a natural part of being a shifter. We simply need to remind your body where to begin. Now try to imagine your human form." Sounded way too easy.

"I don't remember what my human form looked like?" Who remembered what they looked like when they were a child if they didn't have pictures?

"That's okay. We were similar in appearance, so start with the common traits like our white hair, body shape, and size," Sarah suggested, sounding completely logical.

Elena did what her sister suggested. She envisioned Sarah's body shape and long white hair. For some unknown reason, she felt her hair was even longer and added that detail. Pale blue eyes appeared in her vision to match Sarah's, along with a pointed chin. Piece by piece, Elena put herself back together again or at least a close facsimile until she felt confident enough to give it a shot.

"Now reach for that form with all your strength and imagine pulling it on like a shirt or pants." As promised, Sarah was right by her side.

Elena couldn't help but shiver. It sounded as if she were putting on a human skin suit, gross and way too close to what Collector Demons did with humans. *"Yeah, not a stellar comparison."*

"Okay, okay. How about this? Pull the form to you and wrap it around yourself like a warm blanket."

"You should have gone with that one first," Elena teased.

Sarah's laughter bubbled along their link joining her own. Gods, it felt good to laugh again.

She reached for the vision in her mind, but she was having difficulty pulling it to her. One time she could barely move the image, and the next, it came freely but snapped back when it got close to her.

"Keep trying. You'll get it. You're just out of practice." Sarah cheered her on.

Elena wished she had as much faith in herself as Sarah seemed to have in her, but she wasn't a quitter. Soon with each attempt, the vision she'd created of herself moved closer. It was a full-out struggle, but she managed to wrap the vision around herself before closing her eyes.

Muscles stretched and contracted as bones snapped and reset repeatedly. Elena's claws retracted along with her sharp canines, and fur gave way to skin. By the time she'd completed her full shift, Elena had collapsed panting onto the carpet. She felt a blanket being placed over the top of her, and Elena looked back to find Sarah fully dressed and covering her.

She'd done it. After decades of being forced to stay as a hyena to protect herself, she was back in her human form. This form wasn't as strong and resilient as her hyena's but she was safe with her sister.

"How do you feel?" Sarah asked, her voice soft and soothing.

Elena did a quick scan of her body and found no pain. "I-I'm... Okay," she said, coughing. Her voice was scratchy, and she had to force the words out of her mouth instead of using the link. Suddenly, she got the overwhelming urge to know what she looked like and to see how close she'd gotten to her vision. Elena had never expected to see her adult human form but was now excited by it.

Sarah must have sensed her curiosity and went running into the bathroom. Seconds later, she returned with a hand mirror. Elena sat up, unsure if she liked the feel of this fabric against her skin. She'd always had the protection of her fur to prevent rubbing and chaffing.

Elena took the mirror her sister held out with shaky hands and slowly moved it up to her face. White hair fell like waves around her head, partially hiding the scars circling her neck caused by the collar she'd been forced to wear. She wasn't sure how she felt about the marks, but that was an issue she'd have to deal with another time.

Her eyes were more grey than pale blue, and her chin wasn't as pointed, but this reflection was the true her. It was far away from the child, she vaguely remembered, but when she smiled, a hint of recognition struck her making her smile even wider. Of course, her skin was still covered in iridescent lightning bolts, but what else could she have expected, considering she'd overheard they were permanent.

"You're as beautiful as I remember, sis," Sarah said, her voice low and broken with emotion.

Elena set the mirror down and opened her arms to her sister. This would be the first hug they'd shared since that horrible day when everything was taken away from them. The mere thought of it made her shake.

"You are safe here, Elena. You can live your life free here in the bunkers. No one will make you use your powers. It's completely up to you if you do," Sarah explained.

"Do you?" Elena had already used her powers to change the molecular makeup of the blade that the shifter-child was holding to his neck. Turning it from solid metal to metal dust the moment she saw it.

"Yes. We are all fighting to drive the demons back and save who and what's left above ground. I use my powers to help in that cause. I repair things here and help Ben research into what makes the Collectors' technology work." Sarah seemed proud of her contribution.

"I should help them too." Her voice was still rough. "They used that collar on me."

"Me too, sis. However, I believe you've already used those powers by saving that boy's life. I'm so proud of you for that, and I believe the Goddess Isis chose wisely when picking you. Do you want to talk about what happened?" It didn't surprise Elena that her sister knew what she'd done

"Can I take a bath first and find some clothes?" Elena asked, trying to put off the inevitable. "It will help me relax a little."

Sarah smiled at her knowing full well that she was stalling. "Of course. Hope made you some new clothing. She did the same for me when I first arrived. It's all been placed in your dresser."

"That bear-shifter is a saint already. I understand why Hope would be chosen. Me, I'm not so sure about." Elena had to admit they were completely different from one another.

When it looked like Sarah would argue with her comparison, Elena couldn't help but smile and hug her tighter. She had her sister's back as well and swore this time no one was going to separate them again. She'd use all her powers to ensure that.

When she was ready, Elena stood. Dizziness swamped her from the combination of her changed center of gravity, being on only two legs again, and the sightline difference from her height.

"Easy," Sarah said while steadying her. "It might take a bit to get used to this form."

"It feels like I'm learning to walk all over again." Weird.

"After so many years, I imagine it is. How about I come with you and give you a hand until you get your bearings?" Sarah offered.

As her legs continued to wobble, Elena agreed, "I think that's a good idea. To survive this long, only to get taken out by a broken neck slipping in the tub wasn't the way I'd like my life to end. Embarrassing."

"Well, I don't want your life to be ended in any way possible, so that's off the table. I got you back, and I'll be damned if I'm going to lose you again."

Elena pulled her sister closer. It was wonderful they were both on the same page about that. "Don't worry. I have no plans of going anywhere."

"Good," Sarah said. "Now, let's go get you into that tub. You'll feel much better."

Gods, Elena had missed her sister. The more time they spent together, the more memories came rushing back to the surface. There had to be a guardian angel watching over her to bring them back together, and she'd always be grateful.

Chapter Eight

Elena sat on the couch in her apartment with a soft blanket wrapped around herself as the bunker's leaders looked on. The night before, Elena had been so exhausted from the day's events that after her bath, she fell into a deep sleep, and Sarah hadn't woken her. When she stepped out of her bedroom the next morning, Elena had people waiting to speak with her. Considering the triads were among the group, she didn't think it was wise to decline.

So here she sat with Sarah and Joseph sitting on either side of her, which she appreciated more than she could express. Elena wasn't ready to get too close to anyone else in her human form. Both alpha triads were sitting on chairs pulled into her living room from her sister's apartment. Goddess Zahra and the Porda Clan General, John, sat at the far end of the sectional couch along with Hope and Gareth. On the table between them sat the metal dust and the remains of the knife the boy had been holding.

Seeing everyone there was overwhelming, but there was no way she would show fear. She could never show fear. That lesson had been drilled into her a long time ago.

"Thank you for allowing us into your home, Elena," Raz said. "No one is here to hurt you in any way."

Maybe she wasn't pulling off fearless as well as she thought she was.

"During these ever-changing times, it's important for us to move quickly in battle and in the protection of the shifters under our care," Mason explained.

"I understand," Elena agreed. She had to admit there wasn't a trace of anger or animosity in the air. Her voice was much stronger than the night before as her body healed itself, but she still was no conversationalist.

"Can you tell us about your powers and what happens to you when you sense a Deshr?" Rose asked.

Before Elena could say a word, a mishmash of throw pillows came running into the room. Elena lowered her hand and rubbed the pillow puppy on its cotton embroidered head, happy with how this companion had turned out. She'd created him to play with the children and the other real puppy, Archie. After a few moments of scratches, Elena rubbed his head one last time before sending him out to the courtyard to play with the children.

"Is it sentient?" Xander asked as he watched the pillow puppy run back out the door.

"They can be if I allow it." First question down, and probably a million more to go.

"If you allow it?" John asked. "Could you explain that further?"

With a quick glance at Sarah for reassurance, Elena continued. "If it makes sense for the creation to have feelings and be self-aware. Like the pillow puppy, it needed a personality to play like a human dog and make the children happy, so it is sentient now as I intend to care for it."

"And those giant metal creatures back at the facility you were being held in?" Mason continued with the questions. Her former masters had made her create metal beasts, but they were never aware she could make them sentient if she wanted to. The destruction that could have been rained down upon the human and shifter world would have been catastrophic.

"No, I would never wish a creation like that to have choices. They were mere shells. I controlled them. They were made from old and discarded pieces of vehicles and machines."

"So, the puppy has free will?" Raz asked.

"Yes. It can choose when it wants to play and where it goes in the restricted area. However, it does listen to my commands above all else, so there is a failsafe."

"Failsafe?" Axel asked while leaning forward.

"Yes. I can't predict the future, so I have built in the ability for me to control what's created if the need arises. Much like a well-trained dog." That was the best way to describe it in her mind.

Everyone was staring at her like she'd grown another head, making her even more nervous. Would they fear her? After all, she had tried to crush them at their initial meeting. Would they send her away? Or worse, send her and Sarah away? Her sister had a mate and a home here, and Elena didn't want to be the cause of her losing her safety and security. Every thought was worse until she had herself worked up.

"That's amazing," Zahra said, breaking the extended silence. *"No wonder those assholes wanted to control your powers, but here you have a choice. Always remember that."*

She echoed what Sarah had said yesterday, slightly lowering Elena's anxiety level. They didn't appear to want to control her, and she sensed no deceit. This was new.

Hope cleared her throat. "When I sense the Deshrs, my skin begins to tingle, and the fine hair on my arms raise. Soon after my markings begin to glow and I can pinpoint where the creature is hiding," Hope explained. The shifter had always been so kind to Elena, so it didn't surprise her Hope would share what she felt first to ease her worry. It was good to see Gareth holding her hand.

"For me, it's much the same, but I also receive a vision of the area the Deshr is hiding at the time," Elena explained. "But I also get a glimpse inside the beasts."

"What do you mean?" Hope asked.

"The first time it happened I didn't realize it until the second Deshr came along. I get an instant impression; I think that's the word."

"Can you explain these impressions to us?" Rose asked.

"It's almost as if they have a hunger they can't satisfy, endlessly hunting, their excitement at finding their prey, and the anger at being interrupted from their quest." Sarah hoped she was explaining it properly so that they could understand what she was feeling.

"That's helpful," Hope said with a smile. "It's good to know I'm not the only one with the ability to track these creatures. We have so many children to protect in the bunkers. You're like my sister-in-arms."

A warm feeling washed over Elena. She liked the sound of that. To be part of a team would be in stark contrast to her previous life, where she was kept in isolation. Of course, Sarah would always be first in her mind and heart, but maybe there was room for a few more. She'd never had that option before now.

"Do your markings heat up when a Deshr is close?" Elena asked Hope.

"Yes, but the heat never really touches or hurts me," Hope answered. "And great work with the knife." She motioned towards the bladeless hilt still sitting on the table.

"That's exactly how my body feels when it happens," Elena said. She wasn't losing her mind; it was real.

Sarah reached over and took hold of Elena's hand, happily sharing in her joy.

"You saved that young boy," Raz said. "Thank you on behalf of him and his parents, as well as the rest of us."

"Hope was the one to attack the Deshr first," she didn't deserve the praise.

"We appreciate Hope as well and have told her so, but thank you for readily sharing the accolades," Rose responded.

"Elena, do you know much about the collar you were wearing or a device that appears to suck the life force out of a shifter and transfers it into the Collector Demon's host body?" Axel asked while pulling Raz closer. The goddess gave him an indulgent smile.

"I remember someone named Treg when I was a child, and when he appeared again recently, he was using the name Russo. He'd bring things to my captors to test on shifters. They never bothered censoring their conversations around me as I was viewed as nothing more than an illiterate machine. Does that help?"

"Russo? That's the same demon who was leading the Collectors who were operating a shifter zoo of sorts that kidnapped Marie and Ben's mother," Riker growled. "That would mean he's been on this side of the veil between our worlds for decades, possibly centuries before the first obvious attacks on the human world," His words caused Elena to push back deeper into the couch cushions. *Damnit.*

The moment the large beta bear realized her fear, he immediately apologized, "I'm sorry, Elena, I was not angry with you, and I didn't mean to scare you. It's only that that particular demon has caused a great deal of suffering and we'd like to get our hands on him."

She could feel her cheeks warming in embarrassment. *Great, now I'm behaving like a coward.*

"You could never be a coward. You're a survivor," Sarah said through their private sister link. *"I'm so proud of you and the strength you are showing by allowing everyone here while still in your human form."*

"Thank you, sis." She needed that.

"How is that possible?" Rose asked. "Collectors aren't strong enough to retain form without finding a host. If he were hopping from one human shell to another all this time, wouldn't he have been noticed before now?"

"There have been many truly evil individuals in the world over the centuries, so Russo or whatever name he used may have been skipping through hosts all this time. Dictators are known for wearing dark sunglasses when out in public, so no one might have noticed his black eyes."

"He'd have to be extremely strong. He did behave as a leader to the other demons," Raz stated. "Thank you, Elena. That information will help us prepare before we are forced to face him again. Do you think we might talk again in the future about this demon?"

"You're welcome," she said, stuck for anything else to say. "And I'll tell you anything you want to know if it helps."

"You are very much like your sister, who has helped save us a time or two." Raz smiled wide as she motioned towards Sarah.

"So, does this mean all five goddesses have been resurrected and reunited?" Joseph asked. "Will the war now begin?"

Elena could see the nods already starting from the three original goddesses. This was getting out of hand. "I'm not a goddess."

That got everyone's attention, making Elena instantly regret speaking up.

"Why do you say that Elena?" Raz asked, concern evident in her voice.

She squeezed her sister's hand even harder, but Sarah never once pulled back. "I'm not a chosen one. I have nothing left to offer or the ability to lead anybody. The Collectors made sure of that. As you have seen, one growl has me cowering in the cushions when what you need are five leaders, not four plus one scared-of-own-shadow."

It looked like everyone was about to talk, but Raz raised her hand, silencing them all. "We shall see, Elena. Until then, we would appreciate your continued assistance with the Deshrs."

"Of course. I won't allow those creatures to harm innocent children." They'd have to get through her first.

A swift knock made Elena jump even though it wasn't even her door. Considering no one would be visiting her, maybe it was someone looking for one of the triads.

"It's okay, Elena," Sarah reassured as Joseph stood to answer the door. *When will I stop flinching at every noise?*

Elena watched as Joseph opened her door by only a crack so that she couldn't see out. It took mere seconds for the new arrival's scent to reach Elena, and there was something about it that caught her hyena's attention. The animal homed in on it and began pacing back and forth inside of her. The notes of cedar and rich earthy musk had Elena sitting up and taking note.

"What is it, sister?" Sarah asked.

Elena immediately shared her odd reaction through their sister link. Sarah's eyes opened wide, and she was about to ask what was wrong when a growl erupted from the doorway.

"Solomon, what the hell?" Joseph asked but was quickly shoved aside, revealing a large wolf-shifter filling the doorway.

His eyes flashed when they landed on Elena, and he growled out one terrifying word.

"Mate."

***

Solomon wasn't one hundred percent sure what was going on, but his wolf knew one thing, Sarah's sister was his fated mate. A hyena was his mate. Now that he'd gotten over his concerns about Sarah mating his brother, Joseph, it seemed the gods ordained it to have happened to him. Two wolf-shifter brothers mated to two hyena-shifter sisters. Yep, this was a little messed up.

The moment he realized his mate was in that room, Solomon had pushed his brother aside in his excitement. That's as far as he got before Sarah's sister was whisked away, and he was dragged back out of the apartment. He hadn't had the opportunity to visit his brother and Sarah in quite a while due to being stationed at the far end of the bunkers and the many top-side missions he'd been on. So, this was their first meeting. He didn't even know her name, but her fear was obvious. Solomon quickly wrestled back control from his overexcited wolf. He never wanted to scare his fated mate.

The bunker was buzzing with the news of these red demons called Deshrs, and he'd come to speak to his brother about assisting in any way to protect the children. Now he sat in the boardroom waiting for the alpha triads to arrive, while his wolf paced agitated at being taken away from his mate.

He heard the doorknob turn and looked up to watch as everyone filed in. Solomon wasn't picking up any anger or animosity from the group, and his brother came over to sit on his right side. He appreciated the support.

"You must understand, Solomon, this is a difficult time for Elena," Axel said.

"Yes, of course. I swear I didn't mean to scare Elena. It was a shock to me as well." At least he now knew her name was Elena. *Beautiful.*

"No one believes that you would intentionally scare her," Raz assured. "However, now you and your animal halves have met, it will be difficult for the two of you to remain apart. Your brother has proposed a temporary solution that may pave the way to relieving Elena's stress."

Solomon looked over at his brother in question.

"You could stay on the couch in our apartment," Joseph explained. "That way, Elena can get used to you being around, and you'll be close enough to each other to alleviate most of the need to be in proximity. Then we take it from there at a rate that Elena dictates."

He was so happy he threw his arms around his older brother and hugged him. "Thank you for helping me."

"Why were you coming to see me in the first place?" Joseph asked.

"I heard about the Deshrs and wanted to offer my assistance to protect the kids."

"How much do you know?"

Solomon found that odd but answered anyway. "That they're invisible and go after children."

"There are a few things we need you to get up to speed on, and it involves Elena," Rose explained.

"Anything she needs, I'm there for her." The fated mating pull was a bond so strong nothing could break it, not even death. The gods created the perfect person for you, and it was typically reserved for only alpha triads to lead cohesively.

Solomon had no idea why he'd been chosen for such a gift, but he swore if Elena gave him a chance, he wouldn't blow it.

Chapter Nine

The children had been tucked into bed hours ago, and she and Gareth were lying in their own bed trying to relax in front of the television. The attacks were picking up in frequency, and they still hadn't figured a way to keep the Deshrs out of the bunkers. There hadn't been any injuries among the children, but it was simply a matter of time.

Gareth's large arm tightened around her. "You're stressing again."

"Busted," Hope huffed. "How can I not be with everything that's happening around here? Who knows what's next?"

"Next is you and me, wrapped up together under the blankets for some serious cuddling," Gareth playfully teased.

Hope laughed as she was sure Gareth had intended. They hadn't fully mated, and she wasn't sure what she was waiting for. It wasn't as if she didn't love him or believe he loved her. Those emotions were far too strong to hide between them.

Considering Gareth hadn't brought it up either, Hope wondered what he was thinking. With all that was happening around them, why had they been ignoring the elephant in the room? He pretty much lived with them now and slept in her bed. Maybe he didn't want to mate? Maybe he didn't want an instant family. Yes, Hope knew logically that she was blowing this out of proportion, but her emotions were so battered from the Deshrs she couldn't stop herself.

"Why don't you want to mate me?" The words burst from her lips before she could censor them.

Gareth looked stunned, and rightly so. "Who said I didn't want to?"

"Well, you haven't brought it up, and we're kinda living together now, so it makes sense." Doesn't it?

"Yes, we are living together, and I've never been happier," Gareth confirmed before nuzzling the side of her neck.

"Me too."

"You have so much pressure on you from all sides I didn't want to add to that."

"But you do want to be my mate and build a life here with the children?" Hope did not doubt that Gareth loved Jenny and Matthew.

"Yes, sweetheart," he crooned. "Whenever you give me the go-ahead."

Hope smiled wide. "Whatcha doing for the rest of the evening?"

The smoldering look on Gareth's face was enough of an answer, and when he spoke, the tips of his sharp canines peeked out from under his upper lip. "Spending it with my gorgeous mate."

Hope rolled to her side so she was face to face with Gareth. Her new vision allowed her to see him in more blacks, greys, and whites than color. "I love you, mate. It took me a while to see what I had right in front of me. I don't intend ever to let you go."

Gareth's smile revealed more of those lovely canines. He was so damn sexy. "I love you, too, my mate. You and the children are a blessing to me from the gods."

Hope dove in for a kiss while wrapping her arms around Gareth's neck. As they mapped each other's mouths, she reminded herself not to make any loud noises to wake the children. Gareth pulled away, confusing Hope.

"I'll be right back." He whispered before leaping from the bed and going over to lock their bedroom door. His heated look pinned her to the bed as he began stripping out of his t-shirt and shorts. By the time he'd made it back to the bed, he was completely naked, eliciting an appreciative moan from Hope.

"Mine," he growled as he crawled up the bed and over top of her overheated body.

"Mine," she responded before his lips took hers in a punishing kiss full of need and hunger.

Hope heard fabric tearing, and moments later, her tank top was gone. Claws came in handy for more than combat. The gentle rake of Gareth's claws against her skin felt glorious, not strong enough to break the skin but enough to make fire race through her veins. Somewhere along the way, she'd lost her underwear as well and could care less that she'd be repairing them tomorrow.

78

"I'll sew them, my love," Gareth growled. "After all, I'm the one who couldn't control myself long enough for you to take them off. But it was so worth it."

He captured her mouth when she was about to speak, stopping any objection she'd been preparing to lob. Hope allowed her hands to wander through the valleys of his defined muscles, circling his left nipple with her extended claw as he'd done to her. He kept his groans low enough not to wake the children but deep enough to kick her need into high gear.

With every touch or growl, her body craved more. She pushed her body firmly into his hands as they closed over her breast, demanding the attention she desired. The feel of her mate's hard body covering her own and pressing her further into the mattress almost had her begging for more.

"Babe, I love you so damn much," Gareth growled before sucking her nipple into his mouth, lavishing it with a talented tongue.

His free hand continued to roam over her, making its way lower with every pass until his fingers brushed against her labia. Her hips bucked up of their own volition, desperate for his touch while snaking her hand between them to reach her prize. She slid her fingers over the mushroomed head of his cock before wrapping them around his thick shaft.

A soft hiss escaped Gareth's lips, and he pumped his hips a few times. "Yesss."

Moments later, he moved his index finger past her labia and slipped it inside her, making Hope moan in pleasure. His thumb zeroed in on her sensitive clit, rubbing it mercilessly. Soon a second was added, and then a third. By this time, she was lost in a haze of sexual bliss as their pheromones merged into a new scent.

Hope may give off a soft outer appearance, but she was half bear, and the two sides of her agreed they wanted Gareth now. A single move of her legs, along with a shift of Gareth's weight, had the tiger flipped onto his back, so now she was perched on top of him.

She didn't waste a second before leaning down and sucking his thick shaft into her mouth. Gareth's claws shot out from his fingers and dug into the bed as he threw his head back in a silent groan. Hope used her tongue to lick the head's smooth skin while rolling his balls with her free hand. Having the powerful tiger-shifter at her mercy was a heady feeling ratcheting up her own need even further if that were possible.

Slowly she released his cock and crawled up higher on his body until she hovered over him face to face.

"Make love to me, mate me."

Gareth's eyes darkened, and his canines extended to their full-lengths. Hope was flipped over onto her back once again with the grinning man hovering over her. Turnabout was fair play in her books.

"Anything you want, mate," he said but then became serious. "I do love you, Hope. I never thought I'd feel this intense joy ever again. You've given that back to me, along with so much more, and I'd be honored if you accepted me as your mate."

Gareth's eyes filled with emotion as Hope struggled to catch her breath. "I love you, Gareth. Most of my life has been marred in loss, but you bulldozed your way into my life and shared the weight I carry. You brought a lightness and joy I haven't felt with anyone other than the children. I'm so thankful you didn't listen to me when I told you to go away."

"I'm here for good, sweetheart. You don't need to worry about that."

Hope flexed her hips. "Then make love to me, my tiger. I accept you as my mate."

Who knew those words would be like waving a red flag at a bull? Gareth took her lips into a commanding kiss that left her light-headed before moving on to her neck and shoulder, stopping momentarily to nibble at the place on her neck where his mating bite would go.

She wrapped her legs around his hips as Gareth lined up his cock and slid slowly inside of her. Nerves were firing, sending signals of need throughout her body. With every inch, her body felt wave after wave of pleasure until he was fully seated inside of her.

Gareth blanketed her and kissed her deeply as their bodies fully joined for the first time. His passion stoked her own, and soon he pulled his hips back and slid forward faster this time. The pace increased, and Gareth raised to his knees, placed both hands on either of her hips, and held her in place as he used his shifter speed to make her world splinter apart.

The maddening pace held her entranced while her body reveled in the overload of emotions and pleasure Gareth was bringing her.

Hope's orgasm raced through her, and her body squeezed tight around his cock, slowing him in place. She reared up and sank her canines deep into Gareth's shoulder, sparking his orgasm. The second she released his shoulder, he struck with the same voracity. The feel of his canines piercing her skin sent her into another orgasm as Gareth growled out his release.

Hope wasn't sure how long they lay there wrapped around each other, but she did know all the time in the world would never be enough with her mate. As their mating solidified the connection between the two of them, she gained access to every piece that made up Gareth and he as well when it came to her.

No secrets, no way to hide your true self, and she worried he might not like what he found. Instead, he pulled her even closer, dissolving that fear handily with one touch. Yes, this was where she belonged, now and always.

Chapter Ten

Elena was exhausted, and as she sliced her claws through the Deshr floating above the child's bed her body ached. They'd been fighting them off multiple times a day, and tonight was no different. This creature seemed more prepared for them and dodged almost every blow. She was alone in this battle as Hope was busy with another Deshr elsewhere in the bunkers.

The young girl was pinned to the wall in fear while her mother tried to reach her from the doorway to pull her clear of the battle. The Deshr dove at the child, but Elena cut him off sending the squealing beast back into a different corner. The mother took the opportunity to grab her daughter before taking off at a run.

Now she could fight without worrying about protecting the child. She shifted all her attention onto the beast sizing up the best way to end this quickly because she needed to lie down. Elena went with the head-on approach by lunging forward, sharp teeth and claws at the ready.

The Deshr veered right, but she easily shifted using her strong back legs to push her from the wall and onto the demon. By the time they landed on the ground Elena was the only one still alive. These creatures were becoming more brazen and taking bigger risks in order to influence a child. Why?

"I'll take care of the rest," Goddess Rose said as she appeared in the doorway. "I'll have it cleaned up before the family returns. Why don't you go home and get some rest? You look ready to fall over?"

"Thanks, Rose. I'll take you up on that," Elena said before teleporting back to her apartment's bedroom where she shifted and stepped into the shower to clean up.

Once done she fell into bed and drifted off to sleep almost instantly, but her nightmares returned to haunt her rest. These nightmares were growing more bizarre by the day, and she didn't know how to make them stop. They presented like snapshots of someplace she'd never been before, along with Collectors, hyenas, human hunters, and perhaps most frightening, children in chains. When she tried to piece them together, it only succeeded in giving her a headache.

The images she was forced to watch confirmed her suspicion she'd somehow damaged her brain while in captivity, and these were the results – recurring nightmares. Elena could hear children crying and was suddenly surrounded by a group of young children reaching for her and grabbing at her arms and clothes.

She looked around and saw no threat, but the boys and girls were certainly frightened. "What's wrong?" Elena asked repeatedly but to no avail as none answered her back. She closed her eyes and forced herself to think of home and her bed where she was surely sleeping. Elena didn't want anything to do with this nightmare anymore and pushed as hard as she could at that image.

When she opened her eyes again, Elena was back in her bed, safe in her apartment. Everything was quiet and peaceful, a far cry from where she'd been taken in her sleep. Had she sustained any cognitive damage while in the Collectors' possession? Who knew? It was possible and she'd have to discuss this with Jewel when she had time.

She paced the living room floor for over an hour, trying to tire herself out again, hoping if she passed out cold, the nightmares might stay away. She really needed to get some sleep. Elena wanted peace. Hadn't she paid enough to deserve a respite? She pushed harder to wipe her memory of the children's tear-stained cheeks from being forced to stand in rows and the tiny arms and hands reaching for her.

Inhaling deeply brought the irresistible scent of her fated mate to the forefront of her mind easing her headache and filling her with calm. Solomon was staying next door with her sister and Joseph while she grew accustomed to him being around. If she hadn't been held captive most of her life, she was sure she would have responded to a fated mate differently but remaining in the past wasn't going to help her now.

She pulled all the blankets off the couch with a loud huff and brought them over to the wall beside the connecting door between apartments. She crafted a cozy bed before stripping out of her clothing and shifting back into her small white hyena. She'd been practicing shifting multiple times daily since the first time over a week ago.

She lay down on her makeshift bed with her muzzle close to the dividing door. She allowed his scent to flow over her as she closed her eyes and quickly realized it was growing stronger. Then she heard four paws padding closer to the other side of the door.

Solomon must have shifted into his wolf and joined her on the floor. Only a few inches and a metal door stood between them, and Elena felt her eyes growing heavier by the second. She wanted to be near her mate even if she wasn't ready for much more. Maybe there was some way to work this out. She'd have to think on that tomorrow because sleep was mercifully pulling her under into a blissfully quiet rest.

***

Solomon knew the moment Elena fell asleep and thanked the gods for allowing him to provide her with comfort, even if it was only by his scent. There was something wrong with his mate, and he needed to help in some way.

The Deshrs continued to plague the bunkers and shifter parents were requesting transfers to areas closer to the restricted zone to be nearer Elena and Hope, but there wasn't enough room for everyone. The unity of the shifters in the bunkers had grown even stronger, seeing childless shifters vacate their apartments so the children could be closer to protection. Shifter families shared common spaces; often with each family taking one bedroom each.

There had to be a way to prevent the Deshrs from getting in, and Solomon had been using his time testing out different theories with every sighting. He'd studied mechanical engineering many years ago when he was preparing to take a position in one of the pack-owned corporations. They used to own numerous companies all over the world before the demons took over forcing everyone to flee.

Before that, every thirty to forty years, a shifter would have to leave their positions not to draw attention to themselves and their lack of aging. Considering a shifter's one-thousand-year life expectancy meant they lived through multiple human generations, it had to be done. Even though they were shifter-owned businesses, they were out in the human world, and having a CEO who didn't age would get noticed in the new connected society. Sometimes they even had to resort to using makeup and hair coloring to keep up the ruse of getting older. Solomon had a knack for mechanical systems, radio waves, and sound waves and had continued tinkering after he'd left the position. Now he was an Enforcer for the pack. Talk about the juxtaposition between careers. As an Enforcer, he was tasked with protecting the pack and all its members much like a soldier in the army, through any means necessary. He'd been in this position for over ten years now. It wasn't uncommon for a shifter to have multiple careers over their lifetime in all four corners of the world. Heck, he'd been a Venetian gondolier in the late twentieth-century.

Also, he'd once done a stint with the Pony Express back in 1860, he loved horses. With a shifter's long-life expectancy, many had a hand in building the countries they lived in. Solomon remembered sitting down for a beer with Wilbur and Orville Wright around the turn of the twentieth century. A couple of forward-thinking fellows they were.

He pushed his body as closely as possible to the internal door between apartments wanting to make sure Elena rested uninterrupted while he thought things through. It hadn't been long ago that Solomon had challenged his brother over his mating to a hyena-shifter. Hyenas had universally been known for working with the human-hunters, tracking down other shifter species to exterminate. Due to this, it had been hard at first to accept a hyena in the bunkers even though she was an albino shifter and had nothing to do with her brethren's actions. This included killing his and Joseph's parents many years before. Now both had hyena mates and couldn't be happier. Strange but true. Funny how things worked out.

With each Deshr attack, Solomon raced to the small tool shed located in the restricted area where he'd set up his equipment. He had a decibel meter, EMF meter, and multiple other machines designed to send out different frequencies, tones, and vibrations on a varying scale.

With this equipment, he hoped to discover a way to shield the bunkers from the Deshrs. Whatever magic the goddesses used to keep the Collector Demons out wasn't working on the Deshrs. He was determined to find a way to stop this invasion in its tracks. Solomon wouldn't give up trying for the sake of the innocent children at risk and of his exhausted mate.

***

Elena stared at her exterior door leading out into the courtyard. She could hear people talking and the children playing with Archie and the pillow puppy. She'd shifted and dressed in preparation for this but stood rooted to the floor five feet from the locked door. Sure, she'd been out when taking on the Deshrs, but that had been in her hyena form to protect the children. This was different, this was for social reasons and in what she viewed as her much weaker human form open to attack.

The leaders had met her human form the morning after one of the earliest Deshr attacks when they'd come to ask her questions. However, socially, she hadn't expanded those boundaries, but Elena hoped today would be the day she started. In the restricted area alone, she hadn't met Marie, Ben, or Joan, face to face.

She could do this. No one here would harm her in this form. There was no reason to be afraid, but Elena was terrified. She could hear her sister through their link offering to come back from assisting with one of the tractor repairs, but she needed to do this independently as an equal member of the pack, no lesser than those around her.

Elena could sense Solomon out in the courtyard somewhere and was determined to join him to get to know her mate better. She'd held on even in the darkest of times for this moment of freedom. All those decades of being nothing more than a machine to her captors who used her natural-born powers of control over inanimate objects and materials for destruction. With a deep inhale to clear her head, Elena huffed out the last of her doubts, stepped forward, and unlocked the door.

The brightness was the first thing she noticed. She could sense it was daylight above ground, but it felt like the sun's rays were making their way down here. The lighting must be set to the body's natural circadian rhythm to keep all living here on the same rotation as the sun. It made sense to keep everyone healthy and on the same schedule. Elena could imagine the chaos if everyone were left to their own devices. Some would be on the day, while others consider it a night. Being underground could mess with your sense of reality, allowing depression to sneak in and take over. With everyone on the same schedule they retained some semblance of normalcy all the way down here.

The moment her eyes adjusted, she located Solomon, sitting at a table with Ben. His eyes were on her, but he didn't move, respecting Elena's need to take things slowly. His smile widened when she began walking in his direction. He was a large wolf-shifter, and she understood why he performed an Enforcer's duties for the pack protecting all of the members in the bunkers. His sandy blond hair seemed to shine under the lights, and his light brown eyes followed her every move. Solomon's smile was friendly and welcoming, and she knew he was trying to make this as easy as possible for her.

All her attention was centered on the handsome wolf-shifter, which proved to be foolish because she didn't see what was coming towards her from the side. Without warning, one soft pillowy puppy and one not-so-soft, flesh and bone puppy launched onto her to play and taking her to the ground. Two extremely excited children followed, and suddenly she found herself at the bottom of a happy pile. Jenny and Matthew were laughing as the two dogs barked and jumped in their excitement. Who could beat that kind of welcome? Her fear slipped away into laughter.

"I'm sorry, Elena," Hope said as she began lifting the children off her while Solomon took hold of the dogs. "I should have kept a better watch on all of them."

Once she managed to sit back up, Elena could do nothing but laugh. The joy she felt was everything to her.

"Are you hurt, mate?" Solomon asked, looking horrified that she'd been flattened. "I should have made it to you faster to stop the collision before it happened."

The kids' faces were quickly turning sad. No way would she allow that. "I thought it was the best welcome I've ever received."

At her announcement, Jenny and Matthew's smiles returned, and both Hope and Solomon relaxed. Much better.

Her mate easily lifted her and carried her over to a chair set in the courtyard's center. "Are you sure you're unhurt, mate?"

Elena gently stopped his nervous hands in their search for injuries and held them tight. "I am well. Thank you for your concern." Even though Solomon was on his knees, she still had to look up to see his face. "I wanted to come out and visit, but now I feel like I'm part of the wonderful chaos around here."

"You are too kind and sweet," Solomon stated while squeezing her hands.

"I doubt that. At least not anymore." The evil acts she'd committed while controlled by the collar wiped out any good she had in life.

"Yes, you are. Those demons couldn't take that from you."

Solomon seemed so sure that Elena didn't want to ruin the image he had of her. What was wrong with him thinking she was sweet? She glanced over at the table where her mate had been working and noticed various machines lined up.

"What are you working on?" This seemed a safe way to start a conversation as her nerves began crawling back up into her stomach, making it roll.

Solomon stood and held out his hand. She took it and followed him over to the table. Ben smiled in welcome and continued working away on the other side, and when she got a look at what he was holding, she stopped in her tracks. Her mate noticed immediately and followed her sightline to find where she was looking.

"The collar," she whispered. "What are you doing with a collar?" Were they going to put it on her? Was this all a lie? Unconsciously she ran her fingers over the burn scars on her neck caused by that piece of machinery.

Solomon stood in front of her blocking her view of the machine that helped hold her prisoner. He placed his hands on her upper arms and said, "We're trying to figure out a way to turn them off from any distance."

"So they can't be used against a shifter ever again," Ben continued from somewhere behind her mate. "I'm sorry, I should have thought about how this would affect you. I will take it away and work on it someplace else."

Elena didn't want to be the cause of him moving all his research and losing precious time from a necessary discovery. "No. I wish to help."

Solomon looked her in the eyes. "You don't have to go through that, Elena."

"I don't want those awful collars used on anyone else. Maybe there's a way for me to help. At least I need to try. I admit I was thrown off initially because I didn't expect to see one ever again." She should have known better than to jump to conclusions. No one had given her the slightest reservation about her presence in the bunkers. At least not so far.

"If that is truly what you need to do, I will be by your side the entire way," Solomon assured her. He stepped out of her way and pulled a chair out for Elena to sit on. The children and puppies were back to throwing balls and playing fetch while Hope and Gareth sat at a table covered with lunch goodness. She had noticed they liked to eat outside their home in the courtyard.

Once she was seated, he returned to his own, which had many machines in front of it. "What are all those for?" she asked while pointing towards the various-sized metal boxes with lights and dials.

"Hopefully, they will help to keep the Deshrs out of the bunkers if I can figure out the precise frequency that would cause the children to become invisible to the Deshrs so they couldn't be hunted by the evil demons," Solomon answered. "Or even a frequency that repels the Deshrs."

"You're trying to find a way to keep them out?" Elena asked.

"Yes. You and Hope can't keep going on like this. You're both exhausted, and since they are invisible to the rest of us, we are of little help. The children need to be protected, so when Hope mentioned a sharp squeal emanating from the Deshrs when they hovered in the children's rooms, I thought about how the demons communicated and searched for children with sound waves. Much like a bat uses echolocation to avoid danger and find prey in the pitch dark."

"Sound waves? Yes, I've noticed those noises every time. Do you think the beasts are blind to us as most shifters are to them?"

"Yes. I believe they're using a type of ultrasonic sound waves to search for the children, and if we can figure out how to use some sort of sonar jamming against them, we'll have a fighting chance. Tiger moths have species such as the *Bertholdia trigona* that have evolved and are capable of sending out ultrasonic bursts jamming the sonar in bats hunting them."

"That's wonderful. You two have been working on the way to help Hope and me protect the children." That alone gave her insight into her mate's intentions and his priorities.

"I can't take any credit for that. It's all Solomon's doing," Ben said. "I've been busy with the collars and that damn machine that pulls the life out of its victims. I believe I'm close to a breakthrough." It was apparent Solomon was extremely skilled and used that knowledge to help others.

"Between the two of you, we'll be even stronger in a short time from now. So many lives could be saved, giving us a fighting chance against the Collectors and Deshrs." Both men appeared humbled by her assertion. They looked down, and Elena was sure she saw a tinge of red on their cheeks.

"We've had a lot of help on this road," Solomon said. "Prior research has paved our way and given us the ability to work this through. We're working along with other shifters here in the bunkers who are helping us to source material and notes of past discoveries."

"It's been a team effort," Ben agreed.

"Humble and intelligent. Aren't they so dreamy?" An unfamiliar voice from behind Elena startled her, causing her to spring up from her seat and turn to defend herself.

Solomon and Ben quickly blocked the other woman's way. Her blonde hair shone in the overhead lighting, and her brown eyes seemed sad to Elena. The others' growls confused her.

"It's okay. She simply startled me," Elena said. "You can move out of the way." When they didn't, Elena stood on her toes and waved at the woman. "Hello, I'm Elena. It's nice to meet you."

Something changed on the other woman's face, but Elena couldn't pinpoint what it was. All she said was "Raine," and walked away. Elena watched as she headed off to a room far away from the others living in the restricted area closing the door behind her. Weird.

"Is she okay?" Elena asked out of concern for the sad woman.

Both men turned to look at her. "You need to steer clear of Raine," Ben stated before returning to his seat and work.

Solomon placed his hand on her back and led Elena to a set of comfortable lounge chairs. Once she was seated and comfortable, he began explaining.

"Raine is… a human-shifter hybrid like Ben who didn't take to that knowledge well. When they rescued her from a desolate suburb in Florida, I believe, Raine shot Marie first chance she got."

"She must have been so frightened?"

"Marie pulled through very well. Shifters are strong. As part of a mission on the surface, it's expected to come under some sort of threat," Solomon explained.

Elena looked at Solomon in confusion. "I meant for Raine. The poor woman lives through the Collector demon apocalypse like everyone on the surface, only to find out she's half animal, which saved her from being used as a demon shell. To watch as her entire family and friends being destroyed by the demon hordes. I was on the surface while under my master's control and watched the destruction and death first-hand. I know what I'm talking about."

Solomon sat staring at her for a few seconds. "I'm so sorry you had to go through that, Elena. That's horrible."

"Yes, it was, and Raine probably lived through something similar," Elena explained her point of view.

"Yeah, I guess you're right. However, even afterward Raine didn't react well to being rescued and repeatedly verbally attacked others, calling them disgusting animals, in the restricted area and had to even be restrained when she unexpectantly shifted into her anaconda for the first time."

"Anaconda, wow. I've never met an anaconda-shifter before. That had to be scary the first time around."

Solomon slowly raised his hand to cup her cheek. His touch and warmth were intoxicating, so she leaned into his palm. His eyes shifted amber for a few seconds as his wolf came closer to the surface. Her mate was so unbelievably handsome.

"You are a treasure. Your kindness is immeasurable, but I want you to be careful. Raine's turned on us before and tried to endanger your sister's and Joseph's mating."

"How?" Elena asked. Her sister hadn't mentioned anything to her regarding Raine.

"Perhaps it's best if you hear the story from your sister," Solomon said. "But as my fated mate, if you wish to know, I will tell you. I want there to be nothing secret between us."

Her mate kept calling her kind, but he possessed a great deal of those attributes as well. "I will ask my sister, and I agree that secrets are not to be part of our mating. I've lived with a lack of control for too long to tolerate any further."

"Agreed, my mate," Solomon said as he drew her closer into a gentle hug which she enjoyed thoroughly. However, her mind was torn when it came to Raine. The only sense she received from the woman was sadness, and it drew Elena to try to repair it somehow.

She'd have to think on this further.

Chapter Eleven

Alarm raced through Solomon's body, alerting him to the incoming threat of a Deshr. After his initial meeting with his mate, he could now feel her emotions when she sensed a Deshr in the bunkers due to the mating bond solidifying. He sprang up from the temporary bed he'd created beside the connecting door and ran out into the courtyard to his many machines to begin testing his theory. A flash of bright white light came from Elena's and then Hope's apartments, indicating they'd teleported to fight the demon.

When the needles began moving on his screen, Solomon knew the Deshr was squealing out its own sonar pulses as it hunted for the children. Using a transducer, he began sending out his sound pulses, measuring how long it took for the sound waves to bounce back and rotating the frequency while watching for any effect on the Deshr. Echolocation jamming required confusing the Deshr enough it's unable to find its prey, or better yet, giving off predator waves to scare the demons away.

All this was done at frequencies far too high for a normal shifter to sense, even with their enhanced hearing. Solomon added an array of clicks to his pulses and watched as the ultrasonic sound waves spiked. It was affecting the Deshr. Now, he needed to figure out which combinations worked.

He worried about his mate out there fighting these demons and moved faster, desperate to protect her and all the children. There had to be a way to stop them.

***

Elena's wolf dodged the squealing Deshr as it attempted to take her legs out from under her. Hope stood panting on the other side of the child's bedroom, working on a game plan. The battle had already been lengthy, and she wanted it over. The parents and child had been removed from the room by Raz, who Hope called on for help protecting the family while they fought the demon.

"Is it me, or are they getting tougher to kill?" Elena asked Hope through the clan link. *"The first one we took on together wasn't hard at all."*

"It's not you. They are getting stronger with every attack," Hope assured. *"Do you think they share information with one another?"*

"It does seem possible."

Suddenly the Deshr stopped making its telltale squeal for a second and appeared confused as it hovered above them. She had never seen them behave like that before. All too soon, it recovered and charged at Hope, who stood her ground until the last second when she used her shifter speed to turn to the side and rake her bear's claws down the Deshrs' back. The Deshr squealed even louder, and Elena watched as the beast began leaving a trail of black liquid, she assumed was blood, across the trainset on the floor as it tried to flee.

"You're not going anywhere," she growled before lunging at the demon and sinking her sharp claws into its body. Elena felt a sharp pain in her side but refused to let go until the Deshr stopped fighting. She threw the lifeless demon onto the ground before collapsing beside it. This wasn't a good sign. Elena looked down to see the damage to her side and cringed at the gash the Deshr had delivered. Her body was already busy repairing the damage, but she knew she was destined for a trip to the infirmary. Damn.

A short time later, she found herself sitting on a gurney while Jewel cleaned and bandaged her wound. Ouch. Elena didn't complain. She'd been through worse in her time with the human-hunters and demons and spent a lot of her time and strength repairing injuries inflicted by her captors.

"The damage should be healed within twenty-four hours," Jewel said while grabbing another roll of gauze. "Now that I have the chance, I want to thank you personally for fighting so hard to protect the children of the bunkers. You've been a tremendous blessing to all of us."

Elena could feel her cheeks warming, and the words, "thank you," made it out of her mouth as the infirmary door flew open, revealing her mate.

Solomon rushed forward and took her hand. "I'm sorry, mate. I should have been able to find the right frequency to send them out of the bunkers before you were hurt. I swear not to fail you again." He was talking so fast that his words were blending.

Elena was confused. Solomon was blaming himself for her injuries. Why? He had nothing to do with it. However, his sad eyes confirmed he was convinced he had.

"Mate, this is not your fault," she explained while pointing at her side. "The Deshr is the only one to blame for my injuries."

"But what if I'm completely off base about the Deshrs using echolocation to find the children in the bunkers? I could be chasing something that doesn't exist, wasting time and endangering you and Hope."

Elena held his hand and went over everything that had happened in her mind before remembering something important. "Wait, the Deshr did act differently at one point. It seemed confused for a few seconds during our battle and even stopped squealing for a second or two. None of the other Deshrs we've encountered have behaved like this."

Solomon's eyes lit up. "Can you give me a rough estimate of the timing of this event?"

"It was near the end of the battle. The child had already been taken to safety, and we had the demon cornered in the child's bedroom. It seemed to stop in place while its red misty shell pulsed a lighter shade of red."

Solomon's mind looked to be working on this puzzle, so Elena sat quietly after Jewel had finished with her bandages and walked back to her office. There was no way she would disturb him while he worked to figure all of this out. This could be the moment proving his theory was right and perhaps turning the tide in this war with the Deshrs. Without the worry of the red demons' attack, they could concentrate on the Collectors and retaking control of the earth. They could send more search and rescue missions out above ground to help others and find items the bunker needed.

"Do you mind coming with me to look at the charted timeline of my jamming attempts?" Solomon asked before realizing this might not be the best time to ask. "Shit, I'm sorry, you're hurt. How insensitive of me. You must rest before we take that on."

Elena did a once-over and found that her shifter healing was well on its way, and the pain wasn't so severe anymore. "No, I'm good. We can look at it now. The sooner we stop them, the better. Maybe we can ask Hope to help as well."

"Are you sure," Solomon asked while holding her hand to his chest over his heart. "You are the most important person to me. I don't want to rush your healing."

A warmth spread through her at his words. Elena had never been important before simply for herself. Of course, she'd been valuable as a weapon, but that was all. This was different.

"Yes. I'm sure. Who knows, you might figure it all out with this information?"

Solomon brought her hand to his lips, kissing each of her fingers. "Thank you, my mate, for understanding."

"You have a brilliant mind. We need to have a look before my memory becomes clouded," Elena stated.

"Thank you, mate. It means everything to me that you have faith in me."

"Of course, I do." Elena looked over towards Jewel's office. "Is it okay for me to go now, doc?"

"Yeah, I'm all done," Jewel hollered back.

She slid off the gurney, still holding onto Solomon's hand. "Let's go take a look at your charts."

He smiled wide and led her out of the infirmary. His spirit seemed reinvigorated, making her happy because Solomon had been so down when he'd arrived. Elena wanted to support her mate as much as he did with her.

When they arrived back in the restricted area, she was surprised to find there were several people still awake. Her sister and Joseph sat in chairs outside their apartment, along with Hope and Gareth. By the time they made it to Solomon's machines, the others had joined them.

"Are you okay, sis?" Sarah asked as she took Elena into her arms and gently hugged her, careful of her wounds.

"Yes, Jewel said I should be healed within twenty-four hours. But there's something more important than that. Solomon might have figured this jamming stuff out," Elena proudly stated.

"You have?" Ben asked as he and Marie joined them. "That's great."

"Possibly." Solomon rubbed the back of his neck. "We have to compare the events with my readout to determine if the ultrasonic bursts I sent out line up with the unusual Deshr behavior.

"Remember when we were fighting the Deshr, and it suddenly stopped moving and squealing, Hope?" Elena asked with excitement. "That could have been the turning point."

Hope thought about it for a moment before answering, "Yes, I do. The demon seemed confused for a few seconds, faded a bit too."

"Between the two of you, I'm hoping to work out a timeline of events so that I can narrow down what sound pulses and clicks I was using at the time the Deshr stopped. Then I'll try to repeat it when the next one shows up."

"I'm in," Hope answered. "Ask me anything."

Elena watched as the group rallied together in support of her mate's discovery. This was community. Charts were brought out and laid across a nearby table. Lines of varying height, some with large peaks and valleys while others barely moved the needle marking the page.

"These came from the Deshrs," Solomon explained while pointing towards the red lines. "Every squeal and vibration."

Then there were other ones in a different color with both, a long, almost flat line broken up by jagged lines spanning the page's height.

"And this was me," he continued while pointing to the orange, blue, and black lines.

She didn't pretend to understand what they all meant, so instead she recounted the battle step by step as Solomon lined up rulers marking the intervals.

"When we arrived, the Deshr was floating above the child's bed. It hadn't had a chance to begin using its influence, so I grabbed the child out from under the Deshr, and Hope attacked it."

"Yes. And then I called on Raz to take the family to safety, allowing Elena to join the fight. I'd say we fought for over ten minutes before the Deshr froze." Hope provided more pieces to this puzzle.

Everything they told him went onto the pages as Solomon measured between peaks and valleys and recorded notes on time and speed.

"It lasted no more than two to three seconds, but it was noticeable. Shortly after that, I was able to get my claws into the Deshr and take him to the ground," Elena continued with the explanation.

A few minutes had passed as Solomon continued measuring and marking, and then re- measuring again. When his hand stopped, he looked up at Elena, who was standing beside his chair.

"I think we have it narrowed down to three possible variations I can try next time they attack. I'll need the two of you to watch for any noticeable changes in the Deshrs when we try again," Solomon explained.

"You got it," Hope agreed.

"Yes," Elena joined in before yawning wide. Lack of sleep was catching up to her, fast and she was sure having to heal her injury didn't help.

Solomon set his papers down and said, "That's enough for one night. It's time for you to get some rest, mate."

She had to admit that sounded about perfect to her, even if she didn't want her time with her mate to end. The rest of their group said their goodnights before Solomon walked Elena to her door. It had been a long couple of hours since being woken, and she had to admit the healing was now taking all her remaining energy.

"Thank you for your faith in me," Solomon said as they stopped outside her door. "It means everything."

"You don't give yourself enough credit, and from now on, I'll make sure you realize how important your contributions are to all of us," Elena said. "You'll figure it out. I know you will."

Solomon's eyes shined amber as he cupped the side of her face and ran his thumb over her lips. "May I kiss you, mate?"

"I wish you would," she said in all honesty.

Elena didn't have to wait long before her handsome mate lowered his head and took her lips in a gentle kiss that sent excitement racing through her body. His lips were soft as they coaxed hers to open, allowing his tongue in to explore. There was no pressure for more, making her comfortable enough to do her own tentative explorations. Sure, Elena was a woman on the outside, but inside she was still that young girl taken away from her family. That's why she appreciated Solomon's understanding why she needed their mating to go slowly. He never pushed her further than she wanted to go and always asked before doing anything.

Their kiss slowed until they both eventually pulled away. Elena touched her tingling lips, causing her mate to growl softly. "So beautiful."

Her smile began hurting her cheeks. Had she ever smiled so much? "Good night, mate."

"Good night, Elena."

She wasn't sure what came over her, but before she walked through the doorway, Elena pushed up on her tiptoes and stole a quick second kiss before going into her apartment and shutting the door.

Solomon's soft chuckles through the door made her smile even wider. This was what was good in life, and it was hers finally. Elena would never take any of it for granted.

Chapter Twelve

Solomon reviewed the data again but couldn't determine which of the three combinations of pulses and clicks had caused the reaction in the Deshr. This meant he'd have to try all of them the next time one of those red demons attacked. Yes, he was closer to an answer, but as of now, the children were still at risk, along with his mate.

The word 'mate' brought out an entirely new side to Solomon. He was intensely hyper-protective, and keeping his distance was proving to be a match of wills between him and his wolf. The animal knew that Elena was their mate and couldn't understand the holdup.

He'd never imagined finding himself in this position before with a fated mate. A pack wolf being given a fated mate wasn't seen often, and he still didn't know how he deserved one. But on top of that Elena was a goddess, even if she didn't want to believe it herself, and as such deserved a strong and powerful mate to protect her. He'd increased his already rigorous Enforcer strength and skills training and wanted to do everything in his power to provide Elena with support and peace to rest between attacks as a fated mate naturally would.

She was truly an amazing shifter; kind, caring, and strong. When the responsibility for the children's safety was thrust upon her, she rose to the challenge and met the Deshrs head-on. Elena had only recently begun healing from her painful past when she was called on to fight the red demons. She epitomized strength and grace.

"How's it going over here?" Joseph asked as he walked up to the table where Solomon was working and pulled up a chair.

"Good. I have it narrowed down but need to wait to test on a Deshr."

"I wonder if there's a way to capture a Deshr? You know so that you could test your theories without waiting for the assholes to attack a child."

"That would be helpful, brother, but I'm unsure how to even go about setting a trap considering we can't see them," Solomon explained. "But I'd love to find a way."

"Right, and it would be hard to hold them even if we managed to catch one. They'd simply float through the cage bars."

The brothers sat in silence, each considering how to catch the Deshrs. Nothing was jumping to Solomon's mind, but he wouldn't give up.

"How are things with Elena?" Joseph asked.

"Great. She seems to seek out my company now, and conversation isn't hard to come by. We kissed last night before she returned to her apartment." Solomon still felt their soft, hesitant first kiss and how Elena snuck a second before hiding herself away. He had to admit it surprised him as much as it made him happy.

"Sarah says her sister feels calm around you," Joseph said before leaning back in his chair.

That knowledge made Solomon feel ten feet tall. "I'm happy my presence provides her with peace. Of all shifters, Elena truly deserves rest after a life lived as a prisoner."

"The same thing I thought about Sarah when she first arrived."

Solomon felt like a butthead for how he'd acted. "Look, Joseph, I'm sorry for all the shit I caused you and Sarah when she was brought into the bunkers. I shouldn't have said what I did, but the wound left by the killing of our parents was still raw to me.."

Joseph leaned forward and placed his hand on Solomon's shoulder. "You've already apologized multiple times. Both Sarah and I understand your motives and have forgiven you. When it came down to it, you were right by my side when I needed you. That's what matters most."

"I hope Elena is as forgiving when I tell her," Solomon groaned.

Joseph leaned back and crossed his arms. "Well, don't worry about that anymore cause she already knows,"

"What? When? Who?"

"Sarah and Elena were talking over a week ago and discussed the first time she met you."

"And she's still being kind to me and supporting my research." Solomon was shocked.

"Yes, because both sisters understand what brought you to that point. Not to mention the deceitful were-lioness who tried to destroy the bunkers," Joseph growled as he spoke.

"Yeah, I was pretty stupid." He'd fallen for the fear-mongering hook, line, and sinker. The lioness had convinced him Sarah was a threat to the pack because she was a hyena, and hyenas historically worked with human-hunters. Praying on his volatile emotions over his own parents' deaths at the claws of hyenas and the guns of the human-hunters, until Solomon issued an ultimatum and made his brother choose between him and Sarah. He'd been an asshole.

"She fed on your pain. You weren't the only one fooled by that crazy-ass lioness," Joseph tried to assure him.

Solomon felt some of his pressure fade away. Elena knew about his disgraceful behavior and hadn't turned him away. If that weren't further evidence of how special his mate was, nothing would be.

"What are the odds of two sisters being mates to two brothers?" Solomon had considered it multiple times since meeting Elena.

"Pretty damn slim, but I'm thankful for it every day." Joseph smiled wide while glancing back at his and Sarah's apartment. "I wouldn't change a thing."

"You and me, both, brother," Solomon agreed. "You and me, both."

***

Elena could feel her mate's eyes boring into her back as she walked over to join Raine, who was sitting in a lounger all alone at the far end of the courtyard. Solomon hadn't tried to stop her, but his warning was clear that if Raine showed any signs of aggression, he'd be by her side in a heartbeat. Even though she was a hyena, Elena would have a hard time taking on an anaconda, but she doubted the need would arise.

The only emotions she could sense coming off Raine were confusion and a bit of fear. The anaconda-shifter had firm control of her emotions, and Elena doubted many took the time to dig deeper after all the hardship she'd already caused in the bunkers. Maybe it was her being new to the situation that made this clearer to Elena, but whatever it was, she couldn't shut off her concern for the woman and was compelled to act.

Sarah had explained to Elena about what happened between her and Raine that night in the restricted area. Sarah had been sitting in the courtyard with Hope one of the first times Sarah had dared to come out of her apartment since her arrival to the bunkers. Raine had attacked Sarah verbally by making comments about her many scars and questioning how someone like Joseph could ever be attracted to her. Sarah had suffered greatly under a sadistic demon master. Elena felt her anger rise in defense of her sister, but it stopped when she realized Raine had done the exact same thing to Elena when she'd first come out to the courtyard to join the group.

Elena and her sister sat for hours talking over the facts and both were left wondering if it were fear or plain meanness inciting Raine's nasty behavior. What Elena wanted to know was why Raine would say it in the first place. She knew how megalomaniacs behaved, lording their power and superiority over others, real or perceived, but this wasn't the same. Elena did not believe Raine saw herself as better than everyone else. Perhaps it was more of a defense mechanism. Then again, Elena could be way off base and serving herself up as a meal to a massive snake. It was time to see which was true. Was she ruthless or frightened?

Before Elena had a chance to sit down, Raine was on the offensive. "I didn't invite you over here."

"No, you didn't," Elena said before sitting. "How are you today?"

Raine's head whipped around, scanning the area. "Who, me?"

"Yes, you," she replied, and when it looked as if Raine wasn't going to answer, Elena continued. "I'm a bit stiff today from last night's Deshr attack."

"Healed?"

"Yes, thanks for asking. The red jerk got a shot in but paid for it. So, what are your plans for today?"

"Plans?"

"Yes, plans. Would you like to come over for lunch?"

If Raine's eyes could have popped out of her head, they'd be rolling on the floor. "Lunch?"

"Yes, the midday meal. We can get to know each other better, and you can tell me why you came over to speak to me yesterday. Do you like chicken?"

"Yes." Another one-word answer, but it was a beginning.

"Great, I have a whole chicken cooked and in the fridge. My sister likes to leave me food."

Raine looked across the courtyard towards the growing group of onlookers. "Is this a joke?"

Elena waved her hand at the group, causing them to disperse. "No, it's not a joke. I want to be friends."

"Friends?" Raine's head cocked to the side as she watched Elena with her right eyebrow raised. Yep, the anaconda-shifter thought she had lost her mind.

"Yes. You know, people who get together to talk, have coffee, and do things with. Friends. I've heard that having friends could be fun."

Now Raine was looking at her oddly. "Heard? You've never had a friend?"

"Where I was before wasn't overly friendly, and my master barely spoke to me. Mainly, only when he was shouting orders."

"Where were you?" Raine asked.

"Many places. I was often moved from one facility to another. After the first couple years, I stopped keeping track."

"You were a prisoner?"

"Yes, since I was a child. I didn't even know what my human form looked like when I tried to shift for the first time a few weeks ago." Elena stopped and looked down at herself. "I turned out not so bad."

"You were forced to remain in your animal form?" Raine asked, her face scrunched up like she'd tasted something sour.

"No, I chose to stay in my hyena form for safety. Having a stronger form comes in handy. You'll see."

"Handy? I've got this creature inside of me that won't stop talking and arguing."

"She wants out." Made sense.

"Out? You mean like shift the way it happened that one time before?" Raine asked as her eyes widened.

"Yes, but not out of fear, simply for fun. We could go to the farm levels and run in the fields or explore the underground caves. Your anaconda wants to be free, and the two of you need to come to an agreement, or neither will be happy." Elena wondered why this hadn't been explained to her earlier. "Has no one spoke to you about this?"

"No, but I wasn't extremely interested before, so I doubt I'd listen. You're telling me I have to give in to her?" Raine looked terrified.

"So far in your life she's been giving in to you. How is that any different?"

"I was in this body first."

"In truth, you were both first."

"Whatever."

"I understand it was hard being in your position. Not knowing you were this impressive anaconda, with grace and power and to watch the world change around you overnight."

"And everyone in it," Raine whispered, looking off into space with those sad eyes.

"I'm sorry you lost your family and friends, Raine. That had to be excruciating for you, and if you ever need to talk, I'm available anytime. I know what it feels like."

"You watched your grandmother shoot your mom and step-dad?" Raine gave her a withering look.

"Damn, no. I'm so sorry. The demons possess the full humans, and if you believe in souls, theirs were removed in a way." That was serious messed up for poor Raine. "My family and pack were killed by other hyenas working for the human-hunters and demons in order to kidnap my sister and me when we were young."

"My grandma was trying to protect us from my knife-wielding parents at the time," Raine continued with bits of information.

Yep, it kept getting worse. Elena hadn't been wrong. Raine was suffering.

Archie and her pillow puppy came racing over in search of extra attention. They were so well-loved. Raine reared back when the pillow puppy jumped onto her lap.

"It's okay, Raine. He won't hurt you. He wants you to pet him." Elena scratched Archie behind the ears.

"How do you know?" Raine gave the pillows a long look.

Elena pointed towards its waving tassel. "He's wagging his tail."

"Of course, that's his tail. How could I have missed it? Seriously, you people think this is normal?"

"I can make inanimate objects move and follow my orders. That's why I was considered valuable enough to kill my pack. My sister and I were separated after that, and I hadn't seen her until she and the shifters here saved me. Sarah has gone through a lot at the hands of evil."

Elena saw a moment of guilt race across Raine's face, but quickly covered it up. "You made this?" she asked as she tentatively lowered her hand and set it on the top of the puppy's crocheted head. The tassel picked up speed.

"Yes. I created him as a friend for Archie and the children." Elena was proud at how well her creation had adapted to a life of its own.

"Interesting, and how do you control it?" By now, Raine was rubbing the pillows with both hands.

"I don't. Not the way you might be thinking. The pillow puppy has free will to play or not to play, but I'm his *owner,* just the same as any other dog, and he listens to me. Seems like you got yourself a new friend." Elena pointed down at Raine's lap where the pillow-puppy was curled up, enjoying the attention.

It was there but gone in an instant. A genuine smile on Raine's face instead of the gloomy look she held in place all day. This gave Elena an idea.

"Do you like cats?" Everybody needed company.

Chapter Thirteen

"Would you like to watch a movie?" Solomon asked as he cleared the dishes from the table and placed them into the kitchen sink's soapy water. For more than a week now, he'd been having dinner with Elena in her apartment, loving every second he got with his mate. "Or go for a walk?" His mate had experienced another nightmare the previous night, and he wanted to tire her out so that maybe she'd be able to sleep.

"I think a walk sounds nice. Let me get my shoes."

"I'm not done the dishes, so no rush."

Elena came bouncing out of her bedroom with a pair of sandals in her hand. "Let them soak. We can do them after our walk."

He wanted to believe it was her smile or joy that convinced him to step away from the sink, but he hated doing dishes. Whichever was true, he soon found himself outside the apartment heading through the restricted area with a blanket under his arm.

"Do you want to go down directly to the park's level first?" Solomon asked.

"Yes, please. I've never been down there before, and I'm excited to see it." It was easy to see the joy shining on Elena's face, making him feel thankful for thinking of it.

"We'll have to make a list of where you've been so we can keep track and pick new areas for each walk." It would be satisfying to show her everything. They had worked hard to make their underground home more livable for all members.

"Sounds wonderful," she agreed as they passed by Raine's apartment. "Can we ask Raine if she wants to come with us? She doesn't wander far and she might find this fun."

Solomon wasn't sure that was the greatest idea, but he couldn't deny his mate anything. "If you want to. She is welcome to come along."

Elena jumped up and wrapped her arms around Solomon's neck and said, "Thank you for understanding." Then she kissed him more forcefully than she'd ever done before. He loved she was coming out of her shell and feeling comfortable enough to let her true self shine around him.

Jumping down, she headed to Raine's door and knocked. When it opened, his mate stepped inside, making his worry spike as he opened all his senses to makes sure she was safe. One wrong sound or frightening feeling being transmitted from Elena, and he'd be through that door ready to battle the anaconda. Instead, Elena came out with a big smile on her face, followed by Raine, who appeared more subdued. "We're ready for our walk down to the park's level." Elena cheered as she ran to take hold of Solomon's hand. It was so easy to make her happy. It humbled him for all that she had gone through.

How had he deserved such love and light in his life? Solomon would never know, but he'd make sure Elena never regretted being mated to him. How could he have ever thought all hyenas were blood thirty traitors without a conscience? Given that his parents had been killed by hyenas working for the human-hunters, he had good reason, but Solomon had never been so happy to be wrong.

They walked down the corridor on their way to the large stairwell set at this end of the bunker system. The colony had over five-hundred shifters, hybrids, and humans in residence, making for a vast space requirement. Even now, teams were building onto the existing structures to house more rescues.

As they made their way downwards, several shifters stopped to thank Goddess Elena for her help protecting their children. There wasn't one instance his mate didn't include him and his machines in the discussions or introduce Raine, who remained quiet, only nodding her head. He never thought he'd see the day when a hyena and human could walk safely through an installation full of shifters, but here they were.

Solomon didn't sense any animosity coming from Raine but something entirely different he didn't expect, curiosity. He thought he had a read on the anaconda-hybrid; maybe he needed to pay closer attention.

Elena was talking a mile-a-minute, and he was sure his mate was trying to make Raine feel more comfortable. As they arrived in the park, he took in a deep breath filling his lungs with the familiar scents of grass, flowers, trees, and fertile earth.

When they passed through the transition between the metal bunkers and the lush park it felt as if they'd entered another world. Large trees of numerous varieties had been relocated down here, along with new growth trees and bushes. The dark green grass rolled on through the park and over a few shifter-made hills. There were park benches and gazebos scattered throughout for anyone to enjoy.

"Mate, you weren't lying. This place is glorious," Elena said, squeezing his hand even harder. "I want to shift and roll in the grass, please."

"Anything you want," Solomon said, struck by her excitement. Then remembering that Elena probably hadn't been let out of her cage to do things others took for granted. "Anything."

She was bouncing by his side while Raine took at everything around them with wide eyes. "This is incredible."

Elena released Solomon's hand and took hold of Raine's. The anaconda flinched but didn't fight the hold. "We can find a place in the park to sit, and then once you become comfortable, you can let your anaconda out for a little while."

Raine looked horrified. "What if she doesn't allow me to shift back to human? I'd be trapped."

"You can negotiate with her. She is a part of you, after all. Maybe if you agree to let her out more, she'll have no problem releasing control back to you. You and your anaconda are one being. You need to remember that. She isn't some sort of invader like the Collector Demons; your anaconda has been with you from the moment you were conceived."

Elena smiled wide and began pulling Raine forward into the park and through the trees. It always amazed him how the horticulturalists kept the various flora from dying so far underground. Whatever skills they used, it was working. This place grew lusher with each visit.

Other shifters could be seen milling all around. Some picnicking, running, and basking in the recreated sunlight, laughing, and playing to their heart's content. You'd never know they were miles deep underground.

"Right here," Elena said as they came to a stop. "Let's set up here."

Solomon noted there were a few bushes in the area blocking other shifters' view of them. With the added privacy, he noticed a reduction in the stress emanating from Raine. He set the large blanket up, and soon all three were lounging back in the sun.

Elena lay with her head on his outstretched arm, and Raine sat with her head tilted back, and eyes closed, soaking in the pseudo-sun's warmth. She hadn't shown any signs of her previous behavior in the restricted area. No anger, animosity, or mean word to be heard. Solomon couldn't help but wonder what had changed, and the only thing he could think of was his mate's friendship.

Goddess Elena might have been given her powers for more than protecting the children, and Solomon couldn't wait to see what she did next.

***

Elena hadn't felt the sun's rays like this in decades, even if it wasn't the actual sun at all. The way the park had been set up, you would never be able to tell this wasn't real. It felt as if they were above ground spending the end of the day in a park. The sun was going to set soon, and Elena wanted to get in a run.

"Can we shift now?" Her hyena was pacing inside of her, begging for freedom.

"Sure, you can shift whenever you're ready," Solomon said to both her and Raine. He didn't want her to feel like it was a requirement, and Elena loved him even more for it.

"Yes," Elena cheered. "How do you feel about trying to shift, Raine?" There was no way she'd abandon her friend.

"I don't know. I'd need some kinda guarantee I can shift back to human afterward. My anaconda says she will never fight me for control, but how do I know for sure?" There was real fear in Raine's eyes.

Elena didn't know of any guarantee. She looked up at Solomon for help.

"If your anaconda doesn't allow you to shift back, I swear I will call on Goddess Raz to make it so," he said.

Her mate was a genius. "That's wonderful and reassuring, but I doubt your snake will fight you. She's waited patiently all these years," Elena said.

Raine sucked in a deep breath and let it out slowly. With a nod of her head, she said, "Okay, let's give it a try."

"How about you go first, and I'll help you through it. Then I'll shift, and we can go searching through the woods and check out this huge area properly."

"I have to get naked, right?" Raine asked, not looking overly pleased about it.

"Yes, unless you want to tear your clothing, there's no way around it. However, I thought ahead, and these bushes should give you all the privacy you need. Shifters and nudity go hand in hand. We shift so often clothes would never last if we kept tearing them."

"Yeah, not so much in my family. Ultra-conservative types, but I guess my birth father would have grown up differently. Assuming, since my mother and stepfather were possessed, it wasn't my mom who was a shifter."

"I wonder if we could find your father. Maybe send out a message or something?" Elena asked, hoping her mate would know of a way, considering she was new to the bunkers herself.

"Yes," Solomon agreed. "We are in communication with other shifter colonies around the world and can send out a message searching for your father. We could put out information about your mother, where and when you were born, and see if we get a lead."

Raine looked between her and Solomon. "You would do all that for me? Even after all the shitty things I did and said?"

"Of course, we would. The past is the past. What matters is what you do from this point forward," Elena said as she took hold of Raine's hand. "Nothing a few apologies wouldn't fix. You'd be surprised how many would understand if you told them the truth."

"Yeah, I guess my stepfather's advice to 'provide a good offense, and you won't need a defense' was way off. I thought I had to be tough and keep everyone away to survive, even if I was scared out of my mind."

"I can't even imagine the shock and stress all these events have had on you. Your family tries to kill you, demons all over the place, then being rescued by a group of shifters you don't know you can trust. You see people turning into animals in front of you, and then you're told you are one as well. The whole situation is enough to freak out even the toughest person."

"It was all too much too fast. You know?" Raine said as she twisted her free hand in her blonde hair.

Solomon reached around and placed his hand on Raine's shoulder. "I forgive you and completely understand why you did what you did."

Raine looked away but not before Elena caught sight of the tears in her eyes. With a quick wipe of her hands, she cleared them away and said, "Thank you. Now let's get on to this shifting thing. I was scared and angry before when my anaconda came out, so I'm not sure how I did it."

"I remember," Solomon laughed, lightening the mood. "You are one strong anaconda, that's for sure."

"I am?" Raine looked surprised.

"Yes, you are, and if I remember correctly, very impressive."

A small smile tugged at the sides of Raine's lips, and Elena couldn't help but join in. "You got to see her anaconda? No fair. I want to see her," she pouted, but it quickly turned into a smile when both Raine and Solomon laughed.

"Okay, we're willing to try," Raine said, and Elena noticed that Raine included her snake along with her for the first time. "What do we do?"

Elena was excited to let her hyena out to run but resisted her own needs to help Raine through her first conscious shift.

"I'll stand guard and make sure you are not disturbed," Solomon stood and walked several feet away. Her mate was such an amazing shifter it was easy to fall into love with him.

She ushered Raine closer into the bushes and began taking off her own clothing. When Raine stood there, unmoving, Elena stopped. "It's up to you, but I didn't bring any extra clothing with us if you ruin yours. I guess we're almost the same size so you could wear mine, and I could return home in my hyena form."

"You'd give me the clothes off your back?" Raine asked, and when Elena nodded, the anaconda-shifter reached for the hem of her t-shirt and pulled it over her head.

Elena continued, and once her clothes were folded in a neat pile beside the bush, she looked up to find a noticeably uncomfortable Raine. Time to get things moving before she talked herself out of this.

"Okay, I want you to sit on the ground," Elena explained.

"On the ground?" Raine didn't look impressed, but she wasn't reaching for her clothing, so Elena took that as a good sign.

"Yes. You're a snake, and when you shift, it's better if you're close to the ground. I like to go onto my hands and knees to shift into my hyena form. It's however you feel most comfortable."

Raine nodded her head. "Of course, I wasn't thinking, but that makes sense."

Elena believed once something was explained to Raine, she felt much more confident to do it. She'd have to remember that.

Once they were both on the ground, Elena continued. "Now feel your anaconda inside of you, picture it in all its glory. From your large, thin triangular head to your shining scales, not cold but warm to the touch. The stunning pattern and color of those scales identifying you as the apex predator you are."

Raine closed her eyes halfway through her explanation, and Elena watched as green anaconda scales began appearing along Raine's back and sides. Once they appeared, they spread quickly to other parts of her body.

"That's it. Feel her power, her strength, and pull it into you. You are one in spirit, both sides of a coin, together through everything."

Once the shift took over, it wasn't long before Elena was looking up into an impressive set of yellow, slitted eyes. Her forked tongue shot out, scenting the area before lowering her head to Elena's height. Raine wasn't an average anaconda size of seventeen feet and thousands of pounds. She was an upgraded shifter version of at least over forty feet in length and multiple tons of weight.

"You are stunning," Elena said in a hushed tone as she held out her hand to touch the large armor-like scales covering her body. "Absolutely stunning."

Raine's head lowered into Elena's touch. *"Thank you,"* Raine said through the general link all members of the bunkers had.

Elena shifted into her albino hyena and bounced with happiness out to her mate, who hadn't moved from his spot. It felt wonderful, allowing her hyena the freedom to run and play. Two things that she'd never experienced until now.

"You look happy, mate," Solomon said as he reached down to scratch behind her hyena's ear. "Where's Raine?"

She turned around back towards the bushes. *"Are you okay?"*

"Yes, I'm learning how to move all this body. Did I have to be this big?" Elena could hear the laughter in her voice as well as concern. *"It's like pushing a dump truck uphill."*

She inched out from the bushes at a much slower pace than Elena had expected. *"You're overthinking it. Let your anaconda lead the way. She knows what to do."*

"You'll get the hang of it in no time at all," Solomon assured. "Now allow me to shift, and we'll go off on an adventure."

Elena's hyena was all for that. *"Let's do it,"* she cheered as she raced back to Raine. *This is going to be so much fun."*

Chapter Fourteen

Solomon lay in the grass near a lake on the far east side of the park. There was a community of chimpanzee-shifters enjoying a day at the lake who'd welcomed them when they arrived. They seemed friendly enough, though they gave Raine's anaconda a wide berth. If she noticed, she didn't say anything, just continued to explore what the big snake could do. It looked like play, and mainly it was, but with every move, Raine was learning. His mate was helping her through the movements, and it looked as if the anaconda-shifter was picking things up quickly.

Elena had the patience and kindness of a saint. How she could still view herself as unsuitable for the role she'd been given as goddess was heartbreaking. Solomon swore he'd spend his life convincing her of her worth no matter how long it took.

All three were basking in the last few rays of sunlight as day raced towards night when their peaceful moment was shattered. One of the chimpanzee-shifters was yelling for help.

"She's floating away," a young woman screamed in hysterics as multiple people physically restrained her from going into the water. Chimpanzees weren't known to be strong swimmers in either their shifter or human forms. In the distance, he could make out a round baby-sized floaty with an above water hammock drifting further away on the calm surface of the clear water, from the sandy shore. In the hammock sat a laughing infant with curly black hair. The family would never make it. How had the child gotten so far out before they noticed?

Solomon rose to his paws, and his wolf took off at a run heading straight for the water and the child. He was running at full speed when he was passed like he'd been standing still. The large anaconda dove headfirst into the lake faster than he'd ever seen, causing Solomon to stop on the dock with Elena. Now that she wasn't overthinking how to move, Raine's changed body quickly zeroed in on saving the toddler. She was something to behold. All speed and grace. In the distance, he watched as many other shifters came to the water's edge at the call for help.

Anacondas loved the water and spent much of their lives in it, and Raine's anaconda was no different. Her scaled body sliced through the lake with little to no resistance. Elena had shifted back into her human form and was helping keep the child's parents calm.

"Raine will get to her. Don't worry," Elena was saying while rubbing soothing circles across the mother's back, trying to be reassuring. "She'll save your child,"

"But she's an anaconda?" The group was still unsure of the large predator.

"And the best chance your child has at surviving your lapse in judgment by allowing her to drift off in the first place," Elena growled, snapping a few members to attention. His mate wouldn't tolerate others using speciesism to explain away rude behavior. "After all, I am hyena."

The child bobbed up and down on the water, oblivious to the danger surrounding her. He couldn't see the snake, but the anaconda was out there. Suddenly, the child lost its toy over the edge and into the water, and she began leaning over the small hammock in her tube to reach for it. Solomon felt his heart stop.

"Mate, what do we do?" Elena asked through their private link seconds before the child fell in and disappeared under the water.

"No," the child's mother fell to her knees in the sand. Elena had her arms wrapped around the distraught woman as her goddess markings glowed with power.

"Wait, look there," Solomon yelled as he saw small ripples on the surface seconds before the crying child burst from the water, being held in the rings of the anaconda. The remainder of Raine's body remained under the surface, with only her triangular head sitting above, holding the child's toy in her sharp rows of teeth.

"She's safe," Elena shouted, shaking the mother so that she would look up. "Raine saved her."

Carefully, Raine made her way back with the child, and by the time they reached the shore, the little girl had her toy back and was laughing once again. Her parents ran to her and lifted her gently from the safety of Raine's coils. The father looked at Raine for a moment before holding out his hand.

"Thank you for saving our little girl. I owe you my life," he said.

Raine raised her impressive head, stuck out her forked tongue before rubbing the side of her head against the man's hand.

Solomon looked at the scene playing out in front of him. This was all possible because of his mate. Elena was a gift to everyone who met her. If she hadn't seen behind Raine's hostile behavior and befriended her, would this child be alive? Would anyone have been able to swim to the toddler in time? He had his doubts on whether he would have or not, considering the speed needed.

His mate worked in mysterious ways, and Solomon would never doubt her instincts.

***

Elena fell into bed exhausted after an eventful evening at the park. If she were lucky the nightmares would give her the night off. She wasn't lucky. The first scene slammed into her vision as if someone took a picture and inserted it into her nightmares like a viewfinder. Children, always children. Chills raced down her spine. In cages and rooms packed in side by side, the scariest part is that not one of them moved. They all sat on the floor, eyes closed, sitting straight up like they were in some sort of yoga pose she'd seen on her bunker's internal television recently.

Kids weren't quiet. There had to be something wrong, but she couldn't find the reason. The image changed to show a location on a map of sorts, but Elena had no idea where anything was with or without a map, leaving her frustrated. She memorized the geographical markers of the area instead.

More images came of older teens being held in what looked like a covered stockyard reminding her of cattle. Some were exercising in unison, while others walked in perfectly straight lines from one building to another. She caught the red flash as it vanished, and another appeared. Deshrs. Of course. Now that she'd seen one, others were easier to pick out.

A large building stood off to the side, connected to giant metal bins of some sort by multiple pipes and chutes she recognized from her life before being kidnapped. Although she couldn't remember the name of it, she knew it had a purpose. On its side was an old worn-out sign, and she could only make out a few letters. Perhaps an H and an M.

The image flipped again, and she was filled with dread. Now she stood in what could only be described as a hospital room. She walked around the empty bed to look out the window to see what was left outside and if she recognized anything. Skeletal, burned-out buildings stood guard over the destruction below with cars littering the street. A large bridge sat lifeless over a quiet bay. The smell of decay was evident everywhere. It had only been five short years since the Collectors took over, and she couldn't say she liked what the assholes had done with the place.

Elena noted the building she was standing in seemed untouched by the carnage surrounding it. She could make out the stone building's Gothic front entrance meaning she had to be in one of the wings. Not a mark, not even graffiti could be found on the exterior. It felt sterile and out of place against the remainder of whatever city she was in.

Voices could be heard from the corridor, and Elena raced to hide. She'd never been in this part of the nightmare before, so she wasn't certain if they were friends or foe. It didn't take long to figure it out. Two human-hunters with semi-automatic rifles strapped on their backs walked in pushing a gurney containing an unconscious young man who was strapped down. She squeezed her body deeper in her spot behind a low shelf to get a better look through the holes drilled out for unfinished wiring and tore her arm along an exposed nail.

A well-dressed woman walked in. "Put him over closer to the window. We want the client to get a good look at him before the deal." Her extremely high heels clicked on the tiled floor and echoed throughout the room, tap dancing across Elena's last nerve.

What struck Elena as shocking was that she was human, not a Collector Demon. She'd seen many red markings on the back of human-hunters' necks while being held captive. It showed ownership, and both men moving the gurney had those marks in various designs signifying the person you'd have to deal with if you hurt their property. Unfortunately, the woman's hair was far too long for Elena to see any markings on her, but she assumed they were there.

A man walked in, and there was no doubt he was a Collector Demon by his lifeless black eyes and decomposing human shell.

"Let's make this quick," he slurred as his jaw bent at an odd angle, more sideways than down.

"As you can see, this is a perfectly suitable replacement body. Only 19 years old. Younger, stronger, and guaranteed to last longer." She rattled off the attributes as if selling a car.

Elena didn't know for sure what they had planned, but it wasn't hard to figure out, and there was no way she'd stand by for it. However, when she tried to move, she found herself frozen in place. No matter how hard she fought, Elena couldn't move an inch. When she tried her powers, they didn't work.

"Good. This last one was a dud. Too easily injured and no stamina." The man raised his left arm to reveal he was missing a hand.

"Maybe if you treated the bodies better, they'd last much longer," the woman said while typing something into a tablet. "Leave your mark here."

What the hell. Leave his mark? What mark? Did they have some sort of currency or power exchange?

"How dare you speak to me that way, filthy human. I could kill you one the spot." The demon lunged forward.

At the threat, the woman pushed back her hair, revealing a large red tattoo on the side of her neck. The demon not only stopped but took several steps back. The woman was too far away for Elena to get a good look at the design, and it was covered quickly, but by the demon's instantaneous reaction, it had to be someone all-powerful.

"As I said, leave your mark," the woman said while holding out the tablet as if she hadn't come within inches of her death.

The collector vacated the body he was in, allowing what was left to fall to the floor, and hovered above the tablet as a green light blinked three times. By the time it was completed, the used human shell had already turned to dust. "Very good. The body is yours. Do you wish for him to remain unconscious or awake while you remove his soul?"

"Awake." The shadow pulsed as his voice filled the air.

"Very well," she agreed before nodding towards one of the hunters who injected something into the young man's leg before removing the restraints. "We will leave you to your privacy and meet you outside when you are ready to leave."

At that, the three humans left the room as the young man began to wake up. Elena fought at her invisible bonds as the black mist hovered above the human. She wished she could cover her ears when the screaming began, but she was mercifully swept away to another location before having to witness the horrible sight.

This time she was the one who hovered above the woman and men standing down the hallway from the room. The men looked uncomfortable at the screams, but the woman didn't react at all. Stone-cold killer fit.

"We have another customer arriving within the hour. Once he's vacated the room, set it up for the next showing," she commanded while flipping through screens.

"Yes, ma'am," the men said in unison. It was odd to see the human-hunters afraid when she'd feared them all her life.

Elena floated lower and got a brief look at what was on the tablet. To her horror, the woman was flipping through what looked like a database. Pictures of children's faces and statistics on height, eye color, hair color, and so on, but down near the bottom of the screen, worried Elena most. Due dates. Highlighted in red indicating when each child was estimated to be an adult passed puberty.

The screaming abruptly stopped, and moments later, the human who had been on the gurney came walking out of the room as if nothing happened. His black eyes were the only sign he was a collector, and his sick smile confirmed he was a full demon and enjoyed what he'd done. Sick bastard.

"Nice job. This one feels vibrant and strong. I like getting a new one when they've just ended puberty," the demon gloated before grabbing his crotch. "And this upgrade is a bonus."

"Yes, I'm sure," the woman said, still unaffected. "Won't you follow me to the office, and we'll finish up so that the men can clean the room."

"Busy?" the demon asked while rubbing his hands over his new, younger skin.

"Yes, that's why you need to take care of this body," she scolded once again, but this time the demon didn't react. "There isn't an infinite supply."

"I thought there was talk of a breeding program being set up for specific adult pairs?"

Elena wanted to gag at the thought of the humans being raised and treated like cattle. What a turnabout of fortunes.

"Humans are more difficult to deal with than other mammals. There are emotions involved, not simply hormones, and then there's attachment to their young," she explained as they walked away, leaving the human-hunters to deal with the room.

As Elena floated there, she struggled to wrap her mind around what she'd witnessed. Collector Demons raising children into young adults to be harvested as shells for other demons needing a body. This had to be stopped.

Alarm filled her as it always did when a Deshr was in the bunkers, and she snapped upright; the nightmare had vanished, leaving her in her bedroom wide-awake. Looking down she found the same gash on her arm that had been caused by a nail in her nightmare. They were real. Her nightmares were happening out there somewhere. There were children being held like animals to be used as shells for the Collector Demons.

Her Deshr alarm had her shifting and using her god-gifted ability to home in on the demons, teleporting to the location she sensed the Deshr and found herself in a child's bedroom. Toys lay across the floor, and two twin beds sat on opposite walls. Hope appeared seconds later, and both scanned the room, finding no one in it.

The goddesses padded out into the living room area to find a shocking scene. Twin boys roughly around ten years of age stood in the center of the room holding steak knives to each other's chests. Their parents were pleading with them to put down the knives, but each time they moved closer the knives were pushed deeper. *Shit.*

Elena watched as Goddess Raz arrived in the background, ready to take the family to safety once she and Hope took on the Deshr. Only this time, two Deshrs were floating on either side of the boys. Using her powers over materials, Elena removed the knives from the equation by reducing them to their base minerals.

Hope lunged at the Deshr to the left while Elena took the right, and Raz teleported the family to safety. Her target moved at the last second, missing the lethal blow Elena would have delivered, and circled back to take a shot at her.

She felt the blades of the Deshr rake across her back but pushed the pain aside and attacked again, catching the red beast with her claws before it had a chance to strike again and sending it falling to the floor. Elena was about to finish it when the Deshrs began fading in and out. Solomon?

"Mate, are you using your machines?" She reached out to Solomon, hoping it was him causing this scene.

"Yes, is it affecting the Deshr?"

"Yes, there are two of them, and they're both fading like they did last time."

She and Hope stood back as the Deshrs struggled to break free of whatever Solomon was doing on his end. Elena opened her mind to share what she saw with Solomon to help better tune the machines. The more the Deshrs struggled, the more they faded, becoming ever more translucent before falling to the floor lifeless.

"Wow, whatever you did worked. The Deshrs are dead." Elena said as congratulations came in from multiple shifters alerted to the battle through their shared community link. *"I'm so proud of you."*

Elena could feel his happiness, and she shared in his joy. This would change everything. It was a whole new playing field, and this time the Deshrs didn't have the upper hand.

Chapter Fifteen

Elena sat in the boardroom chair between her mate and her sister. She'd never been to this room before and was unsure how to act. She was sitting in front of a large round table that took up a good portion of the room. The walls were painted off white and had several cabinets running along them in a rainbow of colors, bringing the room to life. If she hadn't been there for a meeting with the powers-that-be she might have enjoyed the room but in truth she felt like she was about to pass out; her nerves were shot.

"It'll be okay, mate. You've already met everyone who's going to be in attendance, and I would never allow anything or anyone to harm you." Her sweet mate, Solomon, tried to reassure her.

She reached over and ran her hand along Solomon's strong jaw. "I know that, my mate. What I'm worried about is not remembering enough of my visions to get us to the children. We have to save them."

Hope and Gareth sat beside Solomon, while Joseph and Sarah sat beside her. All their support was invaluable to her.

As Raz had explained it, she'd been receiving visions in her sleep, not nightmares. Making her feel even more guilty she had been shoving them away for weeks, thinking it was nothing more than an overactive mind at night or some sort of damage caused by her captivity. When in truth, the gods were trying to get her attention.

After the last battle, her mate had made quite a few discoveries and felt even more confident about being able to scare off any future Deshrs, freeing up time and energy for other missions.

The door opened, bringing her back from her thoughts. Both triads, along with Zahra and John, walked in and took the remaining seats. They all smiled at her when they sat.

"Thank you for coming to speak with us," Raz said. "We hope today to solidify a plan for reaching and rescuing these children as soon as we can."

"We have confirmed with the construction teams there'll be enough room ready to house our new arrivals by the estimates you've already given us," Axel explained.

"And I have received numerous inquiries from families wanting to help with the orphans," Rose said. "This is a great turning point for the colony. Shifters have viewed humans as the enemy for centuries, and it raises my hopes for our survival into the future that we now work together."

"None of this is going to be easy, but we cannot leave the human children in the hands of the demons," Xander added. "They are innocents caught in the crossfire."

John picked up a remote and aimed it at the wall. A screen appeared and slid down the wall as the lights dimmed. "From what you've already told us, we were able to narrow it down to a few areas. Can you have a look to see if any are familiar?"

The first picture popped up onto the screen. It was a map of somewhere. It wasn't the one they needed.

"No, it's not there," she replied, and a new section of the map appeared. "No."

This went on for minutes, and she was about ready to give up hope when something caught her eye. Elena needed a closer look, so she stood and walked up to the screen. It was the upper right corner of the map that held her attention.

"Can I see that part up there, please?" She asked while pointing at the area.

John enlarged the right corner so she could have a better look. There was a cluster of roads winding together like a snake. She had seen something similar in her vision. The heart-shaped lake and town were also familiar, confirming her suspicions.

"This right here. What is it?" she asked while pointing to a dot on the map.

John zeroed in on that location, and Elena felt the rightness down to her soul. The street view showed the large building she'd seen in her visions with the metal bins and chutes. "What is this?"

"A grain elevator," Solomon provided.

"This is it. That is where the children are," Elena cheered, happy she was able to help save them. "There is a stockyard beside it."

"Are you sure it's the right grain elevator? There have to be thousands across the world," John asked.

"Yes, I am sure. That right there." Elena pointed towards the sign. "This picture must have been taken many years ago because it's pretty beat up now, but the H and M I read are there. Harley and Mumford Grains."

"Then it is there we will go," Mason stated. "We need recon on the area very quickly as we don't want to leave the children in there any longer than we have to."

"I don't know if having been under Deshrs control for an extended period of time will have any lasting side effects on them," Zahra mentioned. *"We'll have to prepare for that."*

"Yes, agreed. The children will have suffered major trauma," Hope agreed. "Matthew is only now starting to talk again."

"Okay, let's make a plan to free these children," Elena cheered. "I can't tell you a better use for my powers." Finally, she'd be able to use her abilities for good and not for whatever her master wanted.

***

After days of planning and recon, they were able to execute their plan. Elena and Hope would take on the Deshrs controlling the children while shifter units led by the alphas, betas, and the general, attacked the facility. Once they had the children freed, Raz, Rose, and Hope would teleport groups of them back to the bunkers. The goddesses would use their powers to keep the children calm enough not to run away into the dark to be recaptured by a demon later.

The mission was to keep the Collectors and their lackeys busy while all the children were whisked away to safety. The bunkers had been prepared for the influx, adding physical needs like beds, food, and clothing and emotional needs from nearly one-hundred shifter volunteers to care for them.

Once that was completed, the goddesses would unite and rid the area of all demons they came upon. They could do this. They had enough warriors and Enforcers to overtake the facility handily, but you could never count your victories too soon when it came to demons.

"Ready?" Solomon asked as he wrapped his arms around her.

Her mate had moved in with her, and they'd never been happier, even without fully mating. That would come down the road when they were ready, but for now, this was their life, and they'd make up the rules as they went along.

"Completely," she answered. "Can't wait to get those kids out of there."

"You and me both," Hope said as she and Gareth joined them. "Let's get this show on the road. The thought of those children being held like that makes me and my bear want to tear things apart."

"Save the hostility for the demons, my love," Gareth said while cupping Hope's cheek. "I'll have your back the entire time."

Solomon would be watching over Elena while she dealt with the Deshrs. Then once that was done, she'd bring out her big guns, and along with her sister, they'd tear that place to the ground so the demons could never use it again.

"Okay, listen up," John's voice boomed over the assembled crowd. "You all know your missions. We all know what's at stake. Protect the children at all times, and work in teams to search out any enemies left standing."

A cheer rose among the large group gathered, pumping everyone up for what was to come. She'd never been prouder to be a shifter than she was at this moment.

"Join hands," Raz ordered. "Are my fellow goddesses ready?" It would take their combined powers to teleport this large of a group.

Elena looked up at Solomon as Raz, Rose, Zahra, and Hope all confirmed. Everyone waited on her reply.

"Are you ready, my goddess?" he asked, and she could feel all his love and pride in her.

A prisoner who became a goddess. Elena raised her head high and, in a voice full of conviction, answered, "Yes."

The world swirled around them as the bunker faded away. She concentrated on the location they'd been shown, and moments later, they appeared in the center of the dark stockyard. The groups quietly dispersed, and it wasn't long before they came up to resistance, and alarm bells started ringing. Elena didn't have to look to make sure Solomon was with her. She could sense him anywhere.

Elena and the other goddesses headed straight to where recon had told them the children were locked up at night. Hunters began firing their weapons at them from above on the elevated walkway, which she and her sister easily deflected back at their owners, assuring they'd never shoot another shifter again.

In the barn, Elena pounced on the first Deshr she saw and didn't stop until she couldn't find another floating in the sky. Quickly, Raz and Rose encircled the group of waking children with one of Rose's gold bands she used for trapping demons and disappeared with the first group. Then she and the others went on to the next building.

More Deshrs kept appearing to retain control over the children, but they were fighting a losing battle. One by one, each building was captured, and the confused children were taken to safety.

Once the final building was empty, Elena turned to find a new arrival stalking them. One that walked on all fours, its fur was burned away, leaving only blackened skin, and it had a skeletal frame with rows of sharp-looking teeth in its overly large mouth.

"Hellhounds," Raz growled.

"Seriously. Now there are hound demons. Do they just pull them out of a hat when needed?" Zahra growled as more began appearing.

Battles raged on around them as they sized up their new opponents. They stood to chest height on her, and their tails doubled as a prehensile spear. Always helpful, *shit.*

"Are all the children gone?" Solomon asked.

"Yes, they've all been teleported to safety. It was a true miracle the way Hope could fill all the children with feelings of calm, safety, and love. It was amazing to see," Raz explained. "The power of motherhood."

"Hope is indeed a powerful goddess for the good guys, with a heart bigger than most," Riker said, and all agreed.

"Then, my remaining sister goddesses, let's show them what we can do," Raz said. Her markings were glowing bright along with her eyes.

Elena looked over at her sister. "Ready to have a bit of fun, sis?"

Sarah brought her hands up in a flourish raising a nearby truck off the ground. "I've been practicing."

"That's my mate," Joseph cheered.

Elena brought her powers to the forefront, no longer concerned about accidentally hurting a child. Raising her hands out to her sides, Elena sent out her command. The sound of metal bending and concrete crumbling began as a building to their left began lifting off the ground, leaving broken pipes exposed, and two of the metal silos began unraveling themselves, spilling old grain far and wide.

Raz joined in, and the ground began to shake as if nature itself was pissed. Rose grew ten times the size of her already large white wolf and took off into the fray searching for the leader. After all, she was the Huntress. Zahra's Eyes of Ra markings floated from her glowing palms and out in front of her. Seconds later, an army of Egyptian soldiers appeared in the flesh, chariots, and all. That was some serious power.

"Destroy the demons and all those helping them harm the children," Zahra ordered, and the army legion cheered before turning to run into battle. Their supernatural battle cry could still be heard long after they'd left.

Elena looked up at her mate. "I love you." That had been the first time she'd said it out loud because she desperately wanted Solomon to know.

He wrapped his arms around her and lifted Elena off her feet while hugging her. "I love you too, my mate. I hadn't wanted to pressure you, so I stayed quiet."

She placed her hands on either side of his head and held Solomon while kissing him in a way she'd been dreaming about, not caring who saw them. She delved deep, exploring and dueling with her mate's tongue, leaving no place unvisited. When she pulled back, Solomon's eyes were still closed, and his lips were turned up into a smile.

"That's what I'm talking about," he said, his voice much deeper than it had been before the kiss.

He lowered her back to the ground as her new creation walked over to join them. It wasn't an overly large creation like her master used to make her create, but the metal beast stood at least two stories high, big enough to kick some demon ass. Its body contained parts of the silo, an old tractor, and various other pieces of farm machinery. Simultaneously, its arms and legs were a combination of conveyors, chutes, electric poles, and beams, wrapped in even more metal sheeting. The building her sister had raised began folding in on itself, making it useless forevermore. She hadn't felt more relieved in days to see the remnants of such an evil facility crumbling around them.

The goddesses ran towards the battle, with their mates by their sides, ensuring their safety. Elena sent her creation to collect a couple of vehicles trying to make a getaway through the field while she and Solomon carried on into melee along with the others.

They came upon a group of hyenas who had two wolves pinned against a wall. Elena commanded the metal beams above them to come down to their aid while Solomon's impressive wolf took on the ones further back. Her hyena was too small to take on full-sized hyenas, but her powers could deal with them handily. Once they'd cleared one area, they moved onto the next and then to the next.

Elena's creation returned carrying the remains of two midsized vehicles under its iron beam arms. She then commanded it to go about dismantling the entire operation without hurting any of its allies. That should keep it busy for a while.

Elena turned in time to see a set of claws ready to strike and prepared for the blow, but it never came. Solomon rammed into the hyena's side and took him to the ground, where he ended the threat. She took a moment to look up from the fighting to find most of the Collectors, hunters, and hyenas on the ground and a good portion of the buildings in the compound torn down.

The last few skirmishes ended quickly, just as the sky was beginning to lighten. How long had they been at this? Ra's army began to disappear now that the battle was over, and Zahra was moving quickly from one injured shifter to the next, using her power to heal. Elena didn't have that gift, but she was glad someone did because there were several shifters on the ground as well.

"Is it over?" she asked after shifting back to her human form. Solomon wrapped his protective arms around her. "We won?"

"Yes, we won this battle, sweetheart," Solomon soothed her frazzled thoughts. It had been a long night.

"The war is another matter entirely," Raz said as she and her mates joined them.

"So now that all five warrior goddesses have returned, what does that mean?" Elena asked. She couldn't be blamed for her lack of knowledge when it came to shifter history considering she'd lived in isolation.

"It is the sign that now we must go on the offensive. Take the fight to them," Raz explained. "It's time for all shifters, hybrids, and humans to unite across the earth with a common goal of ending the demon hordes reign. Sending them back across the veil between worlds and make it permanent this time."

Elena melted back into Solomon's hold as their new reality dawned around them in shades of bronze, orange, and yellow. Birds began singing in the distance, ringing in the new day in stark relief to the destruction surrounding them.

The chaos didn't diminish the beauty one bit. Day and night would rotate in their daily dance across the sky, as they had done since the beginning. On one of those days, the earth would be safe for all those forced underground to surface and revel in the beauty for themselves.

Until then, they would fight for their freedom. Stand up to the tyranny and destroy every vestige of demon control they found. Shifters, hybrids, and humans alike building a new future together for the children they'd saved today and all children everywhere.

This was her vow.

A future for them all.

Epilogue

Raine sat down in her living room, ready to start a movie she'd chosen, and couldn't help but look around at the emptiness of her world. A single glass on the counter, one pair of shoes sitting by the door, and not a single picture or personalization of this space. She had a friend, but Elena was busy saving the world, so she didn't see her every day, but Sarah and Marie had stopped by a couple times to visit. It gave her the opportunity to apologize for her earlier behavior helping with her re-entry into the courtyard and community.

However, almost everyone had a mate or a mate and kids, so their time was limited as well. Raine couldn't help but feel lonely as she spent most of her time alone. She took a long drink from her glass of cabernet sauvignon, thanks to Marie bringing bottles back from the surface on a recent scavenging mission. Raine was happy to be a part of their little community now, and she was learning to deal with her fears and asking for help.

With her finger hovering over the power button on the television remote, Raine was about to turn on the television when she heard a noise coming from her front door. It wasn't a knock per se but more of a rubbing sound. Raine set the remote control and her glass of wine down on the coffee table and got up to see what was making that noise.

Looking out the peephole didn't help as whatever it was appeared shorter than the security feature. She stepped back, around here it could be just about anything. *I'm a big tough anaconda, I can open that door and deal with whatever's out there.* Raine could feel her snake cheering her on. Their relationship was still growing.

Sucking in a deep breath through her nose and slowly letting it out her mouth worked to calm her slightly and she reached for the door handle. The second the door was opened a small creature ran in and began rubbing itself against her legs. On closer inspection she realized the creature was a cat and not any cat, but one created from different sized tan mini throw-pillows and those tiny black velvet pillows you find in the fancy jewelry boxes.

Raine reached down and picked the cat created much in the same way the pillow puppy had been, up to her face. She swore even without conventional eyes and mouth, the cat was looking straight at her before rubbing its face against Raine's quivering chin. She remembered Elena asking her if she liked cats and couldn't believe her friend had taken the time to create a pet to keep her company.

Looking out the doorway and over towards Elena's and Solomon's apartment she found her friend standing looking at her through her bay window. Raine raised the cat closer to her chest and cuddled it close, hoping to convey how much this meant to her. At her friend's happy smile, Raine waved goodbye and closed the door taking her new pet with her.

"Would you like to watch a movie with me," she asked causing the pillow-cat to rub against her even harder. "I'll take that as a yes."

Raine couldn't help but laugh as she sat down and watched her pet do circles on her lap before curling up to get comfortable the same as any cat would. She needed this more than she even knew. Leave it to Elena, with her kind and giving heart, to think of giving this to her for companionship.

"Okay, now don't get scared when the explosions happen, it's an action movie and I'm right here to protect you."

Raine wasn't sure how much her cat understood or how intelligent Elena had created it to be, but when it set its tiny pillow paw on her forearm, she knew they understood each other. She was her pet and companion from that moment forward and she wouldn't have to worry about outliving it.

Raine wasn't sure if it had a gender but she decided on considering her a girl. "What should I name you?"

She took another sip of her wine and considered her options when the name flashed through her mind. "Cloud?"

Another tap from her pet's pillow paw. "Cloud it is. It fits after all; Raine and Cloud. Raincloud," she laughed at how perfect the name was before cuddling in with Cloud for an evening of action movies.

Life was fleeting, and she'd never take these simple joys for granted ever again.

ABOUT THE AUTHOR

Lilli Carlisle lives in the country near Toronto, Canada. She is the mother of two wonderful girls, wife to an amazing man, and servant to the pets in her life, and she's a member of Toronto Romance Writers.

Lilli writes paranormal romance, and believes love should be celebrated and shared. After all, everybody needs a little romance, excitement, intrigue, and passion in their lives.

Connect with Lilli:
IG:@lillicarlisle
FB: lillicarlisleauthor
twitter: @LilliCarlisle

www.BOROUGHSPUBLISHINGGROUP.com

If you enjoyed this book, please write a review. Our authors appreciate the feedback, and it helps future readers find books they love. We welcome your comments and invite you to send them to info@boroughspublishinggroup.com. Follow us on Facebook, Twitter and Instagram, and be sure to sign up for our newsletter for surprises and new releases from your favorite authors.

Are you an aspiring writer? Check out www.boroughspublishinggroup.com/submit and see if we can help you make your dreams come true.

www.ingramcontent.com/pod-product-compliance
Lightning Source LLC
Chambersburg PA
CBHW071316130626
46556CB00004B/1633